"There is one last thing you can do for me, Willa. Kiss me."

Before she could reply his arms tightened around her and pulled her closer, and his mouth descended to hers. She wouldn't have thought it possible, but it was better than her dream.

Unfortunately, the window nearest them crashed inward and the kiss ended with his gasp and her outcry. Hissing smoke quickly filled the room and burned Willa's eyes and the back of her throat.

The smoke grew so thick so fast she lost sight of Jared and cried out his name in fear. She felt his hand grab hers as her head spun.

She had no time to wonder what was happening or who was responsible. She only had a moment to recognize that whoever was after Jared had some-how found him here, and now they were in deep trouble.

Willa! She heard his frantic voice calling out her name just before a profound darkness rushed up to grab her.

CARLA CASSIDY

ENIGMA

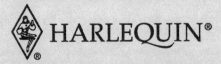

HARLEQUIN®

TORONTO • NEW YORK • LONDON
AMSTERDAM • PARIS • SYDNEY • HAMBURG
STOCKHOLM • ATHENS • TOKYO • MILAN • MADRID
PRAGUE • WARSAW • BUDAPEST • AUCKLAND

Special thanks and acknowledgment to Carla Cassidy for her contribution to the Maximum Men series.

Recycling programs
for this product may
not exist in your area.

ISBN-13: 978-0-373-69466-2

ENIGMA

ABOUT THE AUTHOR

Carla Cassidy is an award-winning author who has written more than fifty novels for Harlequin Books. In 1995, she won Best Silhouette Romance from *RT Book Reviews* for *Anything for Danny*. In 1998, she also won a Career Achievement Award for Best Innovative Series from *RT Book Reviews*.

Carla believes the only thing better than curling up with a good book to read is sitting down at the computer with a good story to write. She's looking forward to writing many more books and bringing hours of pleasure to readers.

Books by Carla Cassidy

CAST OF CHARACTERS

Jared Maddox—A man with no past, special abilities and little hope for a future.

Willa Tyler—A nurse who is suddenly pulled into a fight for her life and her heart.

Kenneth Sykes—A scientist who will stop at nothing to gain power.

Blue—One of three triplets who are scientific experiments programmed to kill.

Jack Maddox—Desperately searching for his twin brother, Jared.

Chapter One

The hospital room was dimly lit and silent except for the faint voices coming from the television mounted on the wall opposite the bed.

Willa Tyler had insisted that the television be on day and night in the room despite the fact that the man in the bed had been in a coma for the past six months. She liked to believe that somewhere in the sleeping recesses of his mind he might hear the sound of laughter from a sitcom and want to join the fun.

Even though it was late and she was officially off duty, she always made his room her last stop before heading home.

She moved silently into the room and for a moment just stood and looked at him. He was something of a miracle patient. He'd been found on the side of the road, more dead than alive after having been hit by a drunk driver.

Nobody had expected him to live through that

first night, but he'd hung on and over the past six months all his physical injuries had healed. But his mind remained asleep and Willa was beginning to wonder if he'd ever wake up again.

"I figured you'd be in here."

Willa turned around and smiled at Nancy Baker, her supervisor. "I wanted to check his vitals one last time before I headed home."

"Girl, you should be spending your time off getting to know some of the handsome bachelors that Grand Forks, North Dakota, has to offer instead of in here with a man who can't even talk to you."

Willa smiled. "Eventually maybe I'll meet some of those bachelors, but in the meantime I've got a date tonight with a good mattress and it's quite possible I'll be there until noon tomorrow."

Nancy smiled. "That sounds good, but you need a little fun in your life, Willa. You're much too pretty and young to spend all your time here at the hospital or in your bed alone. Enjoy your time off and I'll see you Monday morning."

As she disappeared from the doorway Willa approached the man in the bed. He was a bit thin with black hair cut short. She knew that beneath his long-lashed lids, his eyes were a startling blue... but only because she'd been standing next to the doctor when he'd checked John Doe's pupils on a number of occasions.

His features were sharply defined. He had a strong, straight nose, lips that looked as if they might be soft and a firm and slightly square chin. Definitely a handsome man. The doctor had guessed him to be in his late twenties or early thirties.

With a small sigh, Willa checked his vitals, pleased to find them all normal. Nancy had said she shouldn't be spending her free time with a man who couldn't talk to her, but whenever Willa was near John Doe she felt a strange connection to him.

There were moments she imagined she could hear his deep voice in her head, softly whispering her name. It was crazy and she assumed it was because she'd been his nurse for so long.

As a trauma nurse she rarely had long-term care of any patient, but from the moment John Doe had been brought in she'd fought to be part of the team working to keep him alive.

With his vital signs checked there was really nothing more for her to do, but still she lingered next to him. "I wish you'd wake up," she said softly. "You've been sleeping for a very long time."

She fought the impulse to run her hand across his jaw, to gently touch the lips that looked so soft. Instead she straightened the sheet that covered him. "I hope at least you're having pleasant dreams," she whispered close to his ear.

Thank you.

The two simple words burst into her head. Wistful thinking, she thought. She often imagined his voice in her head, thanking her for taking care of him, for talking and spending time with him.

Exhausted from the long day, knowing there was nothing more she could do for him, Willa left his room and headed for the hospital exit.

The warm April night air held a hint of the smell of newly budded flowers and sweet spring grass, a welcome change from the antiseptic scent of the hospital.

She'd only been in Grand Forks, North Dakota, for a year now. She'd moved here from Kansas City following the painful breakup with a man she thought she'd eventually marry.

Pulling her keys from her purse as she approached her car, she shoved thoughts of Paul out of her head. Water under the bridge, she told herself. She'd come here for a fresh start and so far she was pleased with the life she was carving out. She tried not to think about the loneliness that often haunted her.

It took her exactly five minutes to get to the small but cozy house she'd bought when she'd first moved here. Once inside she threw her keys on the kitchen table, pulled the ponytail holder from her shoulder-length blond hair and unbuttoned the top of her pink scrub.

A shower, then bed, she thought. Her feet ached and she was bone weary. She passed through the living room, with its warm earth-tone colors, and into her bedroom.

The double-size bed called to her, but she knew a nice hot shower would unkink tight muscles and make her sleep better. It was far too early on a Friday night to be going to bed, but after a week of long hours she had no desire to stay up.

Within minutes she was naked and standing in the shower beneath a hot spray of water. She loved her work, but there was no question that it could be tense and exhausting. Friday nights she was always ready for a couple of days off.

"The next two days are your own," she muttered to herself as she stepped out of the shower and grabbed the awaiting fluffy towel.

Most of her days off since moving here had been spent working on the house. She'd painted walls, sanded woodwork and had even managed to install a new black sink to replace the old stained white one in the kitchen.

She slid her red silk nightgown over her head and left the bathroom, deciding to forbid herself to work on the house during the next two days. She'd find a park and take a walk, maybe go to the library for some new books to read.

She frowned. Nancy would disapprove of a

solitary walk or curling up with a book as pastimes. But Nancy hadn't had her heart broken by a snake named Paul.

Willa would love to have somebody special in her life, but the next time she'd expect more. She wouldn't settle for a man who held tight to his own heart, who refused to share all the pieces of himself as she shared hers.

She'd make sure he was old enough to have sown all his wild oats and yet young enough, exciting enough, to make her heart beat fast.

Until the moment Paul had broken up with her she hadn't realized that she'd been the one who had done all the giving in the relationship and he had done nothing but take. She hadn't seen the relationship unraveling, hadn't seen the end coming until it was upon her.

She turned on her bedside lamp, then turned off the overhead light and slid into bed, her tired bones melting into the comfortable mattress.

This was one of the loneliest times of the day for her, when she got home from work and had nobody to talk to, nobody to share the events of her day.

Other than her coworkers at the hospital she hadn't made new friends. Willa didn't remember her father, who had walked out on her and her mother when she'd been four, and her mother had passed away five years ago after a long battle with cancer.

Sometimes she thought that the reason she'd stayed with Paul was simply because she hadn't wanted to acknowledge just how alone she was in the world.

You're not alone.

The deep voice whispered in her head and brought with it a measure of comfort. This time she didn't question where the voice came from, only that occasionally it was there.

The first time she'd heard it, about four months ago, she'd thought maybe it was a memory of the voice of her father. Then she'd decided that it was the voice of her patient John Doe. In truth she figured it was probably nothing more than a crazy manifestation of her own loneliness.

She reached up and turned off her lamp, plunging the room into semidarkness as a sliver of illumination from the streetlamp outside drifted into the partially closed curtains. Sleep edged in quickly and she closed her eyes, giving in to it without a fight.

He came out of the darkness, first a tall, lean shadow in her room, then as the light found his face she recognized him as the man she knew as John Doe.

Somewhere in the strange world of slumber, she knew it was a dream, but it felt more real than anything she'd experienced in a very long time.

"You," she whispered. He wore a pair of hospital pants, the pale blue cotton material hanging low on his lean hips. "John."

It didn't occur to her to be afraid as he moved closer. "Not John. My name is Jared," he said. His voice was as deep and rich as she'd imagined it would be.

He sat at the bottom of the bed and reached beneath the blankets and captured one of her feet in his hand. "Your feet hurt," he said and began to massage her with his warm hands. "You've been on them all day."

"How did you know?" she asked as rivulets of warmth raced up her legs at his touch.

He smiled. "I know." His smile was sexy and warmed the blue of his eyes and softened his bold features.

As he reached for her other foot, she thought of all the things she wanted to ask him, but as his hands moved up to her calves and he caressed with slow hot fingers, all her questions fled from her mind.

She didn't want to talk, she just wanted to enjoy this dream of him with her, touching her. When he'd finished stroking her legs, he moved from the foot of the bed to stretch out beside her.

He rose up over her, his blue eyes flaming with desire as he took her lips with his in a kiss that stole her breath with its ravenous hunger.

She met his tongue with hers, loving the taste of him, the scent of him that filled the air. He didn't smell like the hospital; rather he smelled like a fresh clean breeze and a hot, hungry male.

His hands were hot against her silk gown as he stroked down the length of her body. He cupped her breasts through the material and her body responded, arching up to him, wanting more...more.

It was crazy. It was wild, and within minutes he'd removed her nightgown and his mouth moved to capture one of her nipples.

He raised his head to look at her. "You are so beautiful. You've taken such good care of me. I want you, I want to give to you."

His mouth captured hers once again and she was lost in him, in the dream that spun wildly out of control as they made love....

She came awake with a sharp gasp and for a moment was shocked to find herself alone in the bed with her nightgown still on. Glancing around the room, she assured herself that no sexy man stood in the shadows.

"Wow," she muttered aloud and reached to turn on her lamp. She sat up and looked around once again, half expecting John Doe to be sitting in the chair in the corner, or leaning against the wall next to her bed. It had been so real. She'd never had a dream that had felt so real.

A glance at her clock let her know it was just after midnight. Her heart still beat with a quickened rhythm. What a dream. She'd never experienced anything as erotic, as wonderful, before.

She still felt the sweet sensations his caresses had evoked, still burned with the fire of desire.

She ran a hand though her hair and realized that falling back to sleep immediately wasn't an option. Her heart still beat too fast and she definitely needed something cold to drink.

Drawing a deep breath, she swung her legs over the side of the bed and stood, surprised that her body continued to tingle with the residual sensations of his touch.

It had felt so real and in that moment of abrupt awakeness she'd been disappointed to realize it had just been a crazy dream. Maybe Nancy was right and she did need a boyfriend, she thought.

She left her bedroom and walked through the living room to the kitchen, still reeling from the vision of John Doe in her bed. She grabbed a glass from the cabinet and filled it with cold water. She raised it to her lips.

Help me!

The voice thundered. With a startled gasp she dropped the glass. It hit the edge of the sink and shattered into pieces.

She whirled around from the sink and stared around the kitchen, but there was nobody there. She pressed her hands on either side of her head, wondering if she were losing her mind.

She drew a deep steadying breath and cleaned up

the broken glass, careful not to cut herself as she removed the shards from the sink. First the dream and now the voice—his voice inside her head.

What was wrong with her? She leaned against the counter and an urgent tension built up inside her.

You must come to the hospital, Willa. I need you!

She reeled away from the counter as the voice resounded again. Danger. She heard it in the deep timbre of his voice, in the desperate command.

She had to go. She knew it was crazy, but as anxiety pressed tight against her chest she knew she'd never be able to go back to sleep without going to the hospital and checking in on John Doe.

Leaving the kitchen, she raced into her bedroom and pulled a pair of jeans from her dresser drawer. She tugged them on, then grabbed her bra and a light blue sweatshirt and pulled them on, as well.

She had seven hundred dollars tucked into a sock in her drawer. Her mother had always told her to keep a little mad money in the house in case of an emergency.

"Losing your mind is definitely an emergency," Willa muttered as she pulled the bills from her sock and shoved them into the back pocket of her jeans.

As she grabbed her keys from the table and headed outside she wondered if he was dying. She'd heard of strange stories like this, people appearing to other people in visions or dreams just before they passed away. Of course, she'd never heard of one of those apparitions making wild, passionate love to somebody.

The only other explanation was that she really had truly lost her mind.

The night air was chilly and she was grateful for the warmth of the sweatshirt as she got into her car and started the engine.

Hurry! Please hurry.

"I'm doing the best I can," she muttered as she backed out of the driveway. Maybe she should just hurry and check into a psych ward because if she told anybody about this they would definitely think she was nuts. At the moment she would probably agree with them.

Jared. In her dream he'd said his name was Jared. How had her imagination come up with that name? She'd never met anyone named Jared in her life.

She pulled in to the hospital parking lot and the urgency that she'd felt before screamed inside her. She parked and ran for the hospital entrance.

At this time of night the hallways were silent and dim. She hoped she didn't run in to anyone. She didn't want to try to explain what she was doing here.

With each step she took she felt more ridiculous. What was she doing? She was an intelligent, rational human being following a phantom voice in her head in the middle of the night.

Her footsteps slowed as the reality of what she was doing sank in. This was insane. John Doe was in a coma. He couldn't be asking for her help. She'd had a dream and somehow her mind had gotten all scrambled.

Willa! Hurry!

Once again the voice exploded in her head. Urgent. Frantic. And Willa couldn't ignore the sense of alarm that raced through her blood.

She ran to his room and stopped short in the doorway. He lay on the bed just as he had been when she'd left earlier. His eyes were closed, his breathing regular, and aside from feeling like a fool, she felt ridiculously disappointed.

She drew a deep breath to still the race of her heart and moved to his side. His eyes snapped open and she gasped as he grabbed her hand with a firm grip.

"Willa." His deep voice whispered her name as his intense blue eyes bored into hers. "You have to get me out of here. They're going to kill me if you don't."

Chapter Two

Willa's face was as pale as the sheet that covered him and her eyes were wide and a curious blend of gray and green as she stared at him.

Jared Maddox knew he'd shocked her, first by the fact that he was conscious and second by his intense plea, but he didn't have time to explain. He had to get out of here immediately.

He would have walked out on his own, but after six months in a hospital bed he knew he was as weak as a newborn and he desperately needed Willa's help.

"Please," he said as he tightened his fingers around her slender forearm. "You have to help me get out of here. There are people who are hunting me, men who want to destroy me, and they're very near."

He released his grip on her arm and sat up to swing his legs over the side of the bed. That simple movement half exhausted him.

Willa remained frozen at the side of the bed, her pretty features still radiating shock. "Willa, for God's sake, please help me. It's a matter of my life and death."

As he said the words he began to rip out all the wires and tubes that had been connected to him.

"This is a bad idea," she muttered, more to herself than to him. "You shouldn't be leaving the hospital like this."

"Willa, with or without your help, even if I have to crawl out of here, I have to go. Otherwise I'm a dead man."

He wasn't sure if it was his actions or the urgency in his voice that finally snapped her inertia. He was only grateful when she hurried to his side and helped him get the last of the wires unattached from his body.

They were getting closer—the hunters—and Jared knew if he and Willa didn't get out of here immediately he'd be lost.

He got to his feet and would have fallen if she hadn't supported him. His weakness shocked him. It was far worse than he'd anticipated.

"Take me anywhere," he murmured, unmindful of the flap of the hospital gown at his back. "Just get me out of here as quickly as possible." He threw his arm around her shoulder, hating that he had to depend on anyone, but knowing without her help he was definitely a dead man.

Even though he was focused on the danger of the moment, he couldn't help but pick up her thoughts. They screamed in his head.

She was afraid, not so much of him but rather of what she was about to do in taking him out of the hospital. She had questions, too, about who he was and who might be after him. Was he telling the truth or was this some sort of a result of brain injury?

Now wasn't the time for him to answer those questions and he wasn't sure he'd ever tell her the whole truth. The last thing he wanted to do was bring danger to the woman who had been his emotional lifeline while he'd been comatose.

She didn't say a word as she helped him to the hospital-room door. She peeked around the corner and then they left the room and entered the long, dimly lit hallway.

He could smell her, a faint floral scent that was as familiar to him as the sound of his own heartbeat. It was a scent he associated with compassion and tenderness, qualities that had been absent for all of his twenty-eight years except for the past six months.

Neither of them said a word as they slowly made their way toward the exit in the distance. Until the moment when she'd walked in to his hospital room minutes earlier, he'd had no idea what she looked like, but he knew her scent, the gentle touch of her hands, and he also knew many of her innermost thoughts.

Thankfully they encountered nobody else in the hallways. By the time they left the building Jared was beyond exhaustion. It was only sheer determination and desperation that drove him to put one foot in front of the other.

She led him to a car and helped him into the passenger seat and then he watched as she hurried around the front of the car to the other side.

He liked the way she looked. She was tall and slender with light blond hair she'd pulled back into a low ponytail. He suspected he would have thought her beautiful even if she'd been bald and weighed eight hundred pounds because he knew the beauty of her soul.

She slid behind the steering wheel and a cacophony of voices suddenly resounded in his head, the familiar voices of dangerous men. Close. They were so close and getting closer every minute.

"Please, we have to hurry," he urged her. "We have to get away from here."

"I must be out of my mind," she murmured as she jammed the key into the ignition and started the engine. "Buckle up," she demanded as she backed out of the parking space and then changed gears and raced for the hospital exit.

He fumbled with the seat belt and finally managed to get it secured around him as she wheeled out of the parking lot and onto a main road.

Within seconds the voices in his head had faded away and the urgency that had filled him since the moment he'd regained consciousness began to ebb.

He was left with an overwhelming exhaustion. It didn't matter where she took him, at least for now he knew he was safe.

The men who hunted him would find his hospital bed empty and nobody would be able to tell them what had happened to him. If nothing else he'd bought himself some time.

"Where are you taking me?" he asked.

"My house," she said after a moment's hesitation. "It's only about five minutes from here. You can't be by yourself right now. You shouldn't even be out of the hospital." There was more than a little censure in her voice.

"Trust me, the hospital was the last place I needed to be." He leaned back against the headrest and fought the weariness. What he needed more than anything at the moment was a chance to regain some strength and then he needed to try to contact his twin brother.

"You want to tell me what's going on?" she asked as she turned down a tree-lined residential street. "How can you know somebody is after you? You've been in a coma for the past six months."

He raised his head and looked at her, wondering how much he should tell her. As little as possible, he decided. "I just know," he replied and couldn't help the weary sigh that escaped him.

"You're exhausted. You have no business being out of bed," she exclaimed. "And I should have my head examined for having anything to do with all this."

"There's nothing wrong with your head," he replied. "Willa, you just have to trust me."

"How do you know my name?" She cast him a quick sideways glance and then focused back on the road.

"The same way you know mine. The same way I knew I was in danger. It's complicated."

She turned into the driveway of a neat ranch house and with a press of a button the garage door rose. She pulled in to the garage, then unbuckled her seat belt and turned to look at him, the only illumination the light from the garage-door opener in the ceiling of the garage.

"Are you crazy or am I?" she asked softly.

"You're the most sane person I've ever known," he replied. "Can we get inside?" He was irritated to realize he felt slightly faint.

"Of course." She got out of the car and hurried around to his door to help him out. Once again he found himself leaning heavily against her as they walked through the door that led into a cheerful kitchen.

"On the sofa," she commanded as they walked

through the kitchen and into the living room. She guided him to the overstuffed navy sofa, where he collapsed.

"Lie down," she said and went over to a desk where she grabbed a blood pressure cuff. "I want to check your vitals."

"I'm fine. I just need to get my strength back." He plucked at the gown he wore. "And I need to get some clothes."

She said nothing as she took his blood pressure and then checked his pulse. As always he found her simplest of touches not only familiar and comforting, but also more than a little bit provocative.

He thought of what they'd shared hours earlier when he'd invaded her dreams. Hot. And wild. They'd moved together in perfect unison. It had only been a dream but it had been one of the best experiences of his life.

As she stepped back from him he noticed the faint pink of her cheeks, as if she, too, was remembering her dream. "Your vitals are all good."

"I feel fine. I'm just incredibly tired."

"I'll get you a pillow and blanket. You need to rest and then in the morning you're going to answer some questions." As she left the living room and went down the hallway, he felt her fear, this time not just for him but of him.

She returned a moment later carrying a sheet,

blanket and pillow. He stood as she efficiently made the sofa into a bed for him for the night. When she was finished he sat back down. "Willa, you don't have to be afraid of me. I'd never hurt you. Your voice, your touch, was what pulled me through the darkness."

Her eyes searched his as if she could find all the answers to her questions there. "We weren't sure you'd make it back. When they first brought you in we didn't think you'd last through the night. But I hoped..." She let her voice trail off and again her cheeks filled with color.

"I know, and it was your hope that made the difference." He knew his words pleased her. He also knew that the connection she'd felt for him had been more than patient and nurse.

In a perfect world he would have loved to explore the crazy connection they shared. He would have loved to pursue a normal relationship with her, but this wasn't a perfect world and he wasn't a normal man.

"There's a twenty-four-hour discount store two blocks from here. I'll go now and pick up some clothes for you," she said. "Will you be okay here alone for thirty minutes or so?"

"I'll be fine, but shouldn't you get some sleep?" he asked.

"Right now I'm too wound up to sleep," she replied. "I'll get you some things you need and then we'll figure everything else out in the morning."

"Willa, thank you."

For the first time since she'd walked into his hospital room she smiled and it was just as he'd imagined—warm and inviting and lovely. "Don't thank me yet. I still think that sometime between the time I left work and the time I walked back into your room I went completely and totally crazy."

She walked back into the kitchen and he heard her grab her purse from the counter, then a moment later the sound of the garage door opening and then closing.

Jared listened to the sounds of the house, so different than the noise in the hospital. Rest. He needed to rest and get his strength back as quickly as possible. The men who were after him wouldn't just go away.

Somehow they'd figured out that the John Doe in the hospital in Grand Forks was the man they sought. They knew he was in the area and he wouldn't be safe until he could get far away and even then safety was just a desirable fantasy. Why it had taken them so long to find him, he wasn't sure. But now that they had, they wouldn't give up.

Willa. Thoughts of her jumped back into his mind. He'd told her the truth when he'd said that she'd been what had brought him through the darkness of the coma. He'd not only looked forward to her gentle touch and the pleasant scent of her perfume, but also the sound of her voice as she spoke to him and her thoughts that were both exciting and interesting in their very normalcy.

He would have loved to pursue something with her, something deep and meaningful, something hot and wild and like nothing he'd ever experienced before, but he was afraid for her. He brought nothing but danger to her and he couldn't forget that.

He closed his eyes and wondered if he would ever be safe, if he would ever know what normal felt like.

THREE O'CLOCK in the morning and she was in a store getting clothes for a man who had just come out of a six-month coma and insisted bad men were after him. She had to be out of her mind.

Willa pushed the shopping cart toward the men's jeans section and hoped she guessed his size right. She could have waited until morning to do this, but she'd needed to get away from him for a few minutes and besides, she hadn't wanted to see him in the morning with that skimpy butt-baring hospital gown. "And what a fine butt it is," she muttered as she grabbed two pair of jeans that she thought would fit him.

Was he really in some kind of danger or was he delusional? she wondered as she headed to the

T-shirts. She tossed a packet of three T-shirts in different colors into her basket and then frowned as she thought about underwear.

Boxers or briefs?

Briefs.

A gasp escaped her. It was definitely his voice she heard in her head. It was as if he stood next to her in the store and whispered in her ear.

And it wasn't the first time he'd been inside her head. She grabbed a packet of briefs off the shelf and then hurried toward the checkout.

She felt as if she'd stepped into the middle of some sort of science-fiction flick. The only problem was the movie was halfway over and nobody would explain to her what she'd missed.

She'd never really believed in psychic abilities like mental telepathy and precognition. She never looked up in the sky for UFOs or worried about seven years of bad luck if she broke a mirror.

She was rooted in reality, with no flights of fancy, and yet she knew with an unsettling certainty that somehow he was able to communicate with her inside her head.

Had the dream been real? Had he somehow really been with her in her bedroom, made love to her through some sort of spirit world?

Her cheeks burned with her blush as she paid for her purchases. Funny, she didn't even consider paying with a credit card because she knew charge card transactions could be traced. She'd already half bought in to his assertion that somebody evil was after him.

She had just gotten into her car and started the engine when her cell phone rang. She jumped and grabbed it from her purse and looked at the caller ID. It was the hospital.

Play dumb. Please, don't tell. The words thundered in her head.

She shut off the car engine and drew a deep breath. "Don't worry," she said dryly. There was no way she could say anything about what happened. Jared would potentially be put in danger, but she'd definitely lose her job and be locked up in a mental ward.

She answered the phone, trying to make her hello sound groggy, as if she'd been asleep for hours.

"Willa, it's Casey." Casey Durham was the night supervisor on the floor. "Where are you?"

"Where do you think I am? At home, in bed." The lie tasted badly on her tongue. She wasn't used to lying to anyone.

"Sorry to wake you, but I thought you'd like to know."

"Know what?"

"You're never going to believe what's happened. A man came in and said he thought our

John Doe might be a relative of his. I took him to John Doe's room and he was gone."

"Who was gone?" Willa asked, as if confused.

"John Doe. His bed was empty and he was nowhere to be found."

"What?" Willa tried to inject shock into her voice. "How is that possible? He was in a coma! What do you think happened?"

"I have no idea. The doctors are speculating that maybe he came out of his coma and didn't know where he was and somehow stumbled outside the building. Security is checking the immediate area. I just knew you'd want to know what's happened."

"Wow, I'm just stunned. Thanks for calling me. Oh, what about the man who said he thought he knew John Doe. What happened to him?"

"I don't know. I guess he took off. Too bad we don't have security cameras. Anyway, things should be calmed down by the time you come in on Monday morning. Maybe by that time we'll have located our John Doe. The good news is it looks like he woke up. I know that's what you'd hoped for."

"Thanks again, Casey." Willa shut her phone and dropped it back in her purse. A faint chill walked up her spine.

Jared had told her somebody was coming for

him and somebody had shown up. He'd known her name before she'd told it to him and she'd known his from a dream.

Was he truly in danger? Who was the man who had shown up to ask about him and what did that man have to do with him?

She started the car and pulled out of the parking lot. Maybe she was still asleep. Maybe this was just an intensely vivid dream. Perhaps there was no man on her sofa and she was still in her own bed and not driving through the middle of the night checking her rearview mirror to see if she were being followed.

"Are you there?" she asked softly and waited for the voice in her head to respond. There was no answering reply.

She gripped the steering wheel more tightly in her hands and once again wondered if she'd had some sort of psychotic snap with reality.

Within minutes she was once again parked in her garage. She carried her purchases into the house and set the bag on the table.

He was on the sofa, sleeping so soundly he didn't stir when she drew close. Real. He was as real as the beat of her heart, as the ticking of the clock on the fireplace mantel.

He was so still that if it wasn't for the steady rise and fall of his chest she might have thought him dead. Questions whirled around in her head but she knew that none of them would be answered tonight.

As the adrenaline that had pumped through her since the moment she'd awakened from her erotic dream began to leave her, she realized she was exhausted.

She went into her bedroom and changed back into her nightgown and then got into bed. There was a stranger in her house and yet she wasn't afraid. She believed him when he said he wouldn't harm her. Not only did he have no reason to want to hurt her, but he also wasn't strong enough to do much of anything.

The truth was she wasn't afraid of him because as crazy as it seemed, as wild as the night had been, she trusted him like she'd never trusted anyone else in her life.

She fell asleep wondering what the morning would bring and awakened just after seven to the sound of birds singing outside her window.

As she remembered all that had transpired the night before, she jumped out of bed and ran into the living room, her heart pounding when she saw the empty sofa.

It was only when she smelled the scent of fresh-brewed coffee that filled the air that she realized her patient was already up.

She hurried into the kitchen and found him showered and dressed in one of the pairs of jeans and a navy T-shirt she'd bought. He had his long fingers wrapped around a mug of coffee and he looked stronger, more vital than he had the night before.

His amazing blue eyes lit with pleasure at the sight of her and she remembered she was clad only in her skimpy nightgown. "Good morning," he said.

"Good morning," she replied. "I'm just going to take a quick shower and dress and I'll be right back."

As she hurried down the hallway her cheeks burned. She hadn't missed the way his gaze had slid down the length of her, not just with a heady heat, but with a sweet familiarity. It was disconcerting.

It was oddly exciting.

Answers. That was what she needed more than anything today, and she was going to get them from him or she was going to drive him straight back to the hospital and ask for a psychiatric evaluation for him and maybe one for herself, as well.

Dressed in a pair of jeans and a bright yellow T-shirt, she finally left the bathroom and returned to the kitchen. He sat in the same place where he'd been when she'd left.

"Do you have a computer with Internet access?" he asked, then frowned in obvious confusion. "I don't know anything about computers, but something is telling me I need one."

"I have one," she replied, as confused as he looked by everything that was happening.

"I need to use it and try to contact my brother."

"Your brother?" She looked at him in surprise. Everyone in the hospital had speculated about the family members of their John Doe. They'd all wondered why nobody had reported him missing, why nobody had shown up to claim him.

He nodded. "My twin brother. He probably thinks I'm dead and I hope he's still alive. If he is, it's important that I contact him immediately."

She walked over to the cabinet, pulled out a cup and then poured herself a cup of coffee and joined him at the table. "Before we even talk about that, I need some answers."

He'd been attractive when he'd been comatose, but alive and animated he was devastatingly handsome. His intense blue eyes held hers in a gaze that made it impossible for her to look away.

"There are some things I can't share with you," he began. "Knowing too much could put you in real danger."

"I'm already in danger of losing my job if anyone finds out what I've done," she replied. And her job was all that she had, she thought. There was nobody in her life who cared about her except the coworkers who respected and liked her. "I think I deserve to know what's going on."

He leaned back in the chair and cast his gaze out her window, where spring flowers bloomed in lush colors. Although too thin and still pale from his convalescence, there was a simmering energy about him that caused a similar energy inside her.

He turned back to look at her. *You know part of what you need to know about me.* The words were as clear in her head as if he'd spoken, but his lips hadn't moved.

"How do you do that?" she asked.

"It's a gift…or a curse, depending on how you look at it. Mental telepathy."

"So you can read my mind?" The idea was both intriguing and appalling.

He smiled and nodded. "Your thoughts are what got me through the past six months. Your desire for me to live became my own."

She stared at him and tried to remember every thought that had entered her head during the past six months. Most of them had probably been boring, but some of them had been intensely personal and not intended for anyone else to know.

"Are you doing it now?" she asked warily. She began a mental litany of the presidents of the United States, something she'd learned in sixth grade and somehow had never forgotten. Washington. Adams. Jefferson. Madison. Monroe.

He laughed and the sound of it was so deep and

so sexy that a wave of heat swept through her. "That's an effective way to block me. I promise I won't get into your head anymore without your permission unless it's absolutely necessary."

The promise gave her a little comfort. "Who are the men who are after you?"

Her question instantly doused the light of the smile that had lit his features. "Men who want to hurt me. That's all you need to know about them."

She could tell by the shuttered darkness of his eyes that he would tell her no more about the men who were looking for him. "Before we do anything you need something to eat," she said and got up from the table. "I'll fix you a scrambled egg and a dry piece of toast. You have to go easy because you aren't used to solid foods."

It took her only minutes to fix the breakfast. He was silent as she worked, his gaze once again out the window. She wished she could read his mind, be privy to his innermost thoughts as he'd been with hers.

What was his plan? Where was he going from here and where was he from? He really hadn't answered any of her questions to her satisfaction.

She was shocked by the sadness that filled her as she realized it was possible within hours he could be gone from her home, from her life.

He'd been her life for the past six months. He'd been the first thing she'd thought of when waking in the morning and the last thing she'd thought of before she closed her eyes to sleep at night. He'd helped the loneliness that had plagued her since she'd moved to Grand Forks.

She wanted him well, she told herself as she placed the plate with the scrambled egg and the piece of toast in front of him. She wanted him well and on his way back to his life. But she'd hoped for a little time to get to know him before she sent him on his way.

She realized that in the past six months she'd done the unthinkable for a nurse, she'd become personally involved with a patient.

"Won't your parents be worried about you?" she asked as he ate.

He shook his head. "They died when my brother and I were five."

"Oh, I'm sorry," she said.

He gave her a quick smile. "Yeah, me, too." He finished the last of the toast and then pushed his plate aside. "Could I use your computer now?" Once again there was an intensity in his eyes, a thrum of energy in the air that felt urgent and desperate.

She had no idea if the danger he spoke of was real or imagined, but it was obvious he believed it was real and far too close for his comfort, and suddenly she was more than just a little bit afraid.

Chapter Three

She led him down the hallway to a bedroom he knew wasn't where she slept, but rather a guest room where a computer was set up on a small desk in a corner.

Jared had known fear when he'd come out of the coma and realized he needed to get out of the hospital, needed to get away before the men came for him. But, it was nothing compared to the terror he felt now as he eyed the computer.

He and his twin brother, Jack, had never gone so long without communication. Throughout the hell that they had both suffered for so many years, the mental telepathy they'd shared had kept them strong, had kept them alive and sharing the hope that someday their lives would be different.

But he could pick up nothing now, had not been able to communicate with his brother at all since the moment he'd come out of the coma.

Of course their telepathy power had never been tested by physical distance and Jared didn't have any idea where Jack might be at the moment. He also didn't know how the weakness in his body might have weakened his ability to reach out mentally.

What if Jack was dead? What if he hadn't managed to escape on that November night six months ago? The last time Jared had seen his brother was when the two of them had managed to escape from the place that had been their home—their prison— for fifteen long years.

They had burst out into the cold winter night and silently agreed that they should split up in order to better their odds of getting away.

He now closed his eyes and thought of that final moment with his brother. The night air had been bracing, but welcome after the years of stale forced air through decrepit ventilation systems.

He and Jack had gripped hands in a shake they both knew might be the last time they touched, the last time they ever saw each other, and then Jack had turned and run in one direction and Jared had taken off in the other.

"Jared? Are you okay? Do you need to lie down?"

Willa's concerned voice pulled him from his memories and he opened his eyes and shook his head. "No, I'm fine." He gestured her to the chair in front of the computer and as she sat he stood just behind her.

They waited, not speaking as she powered up the computer. Once it was up and running she turned and looked at him expectantly. "Your brother? What's his name?"

He shook his head. "We won't be able to find him using his name. We need to look for a Web site with an eight-point star." He had no idea how he knew this, the information was just a thunder in his veins, a compulsion that had to be followed.

She frowned. "That's pretty vague. You don't have anything more specific?"

"If he's alive, then we'll find what I'm looking for," he replied. Tension rippled through him as she typed in the words *eight-point star* and then hit Search.

Immediately results began to fill the screen. How to make an origami star, how to quilt a star pattern, what do stars mean—all of them results that had nothing to do with what he somehow knew he sought.

If he couldn't contact Jack then he didn't know what he would do, where he would go. The only thing he knew with certainty was that he would not be able to remain here with Willa.

Sooner or later somebody would remember how involved she had been with John Doe. Sooner or later somebody might realize he couldn't have left the hospital under his own steam and might put two and two together.

"It has to be here," he said in desperation. "There!" he exclaimed and pointed to the search result that simply said *eight-pointed star.* "Click on that and let's see what it is."

She clicked on it and the page filled the screen. "It's nothing," she said. "It's just a picture of a star."

"If it's what I hope it is, then it's proof that my brother got out alive," he replied.

She looked up at him, her eyes radiating with more questions. "Got out of where alive?"

He ignored her question and pointed to a small icon in the corner of the page. "Look, there's a place to e-mail a message. Type in 'birthday parties at the beach are the very best' and leave your cell phone number."

For a long moment she held his gaze. "Please," he said softly. "Just type it in and send it."

She returned her attention to the screen and did as he asked and then whirled around in the chair to face him once again. "Now what?"

"We wait," he replied. He had no idea if the Web site belonged to Jack, didn't know how frequently it was monitored. He wasn't even sure how he had known to look for it. He only knew that if it was Jack's site and if his brother read the e-mail, then he would know by the message that it was Jared attempting to get in touch with him.

There was no soft, warm light in Willa's eyes as

she gazed at him. Instead her eyes shone with a determination that was slightly daunting. "Fine, then while we wait you're going to tell me what's going on." She rose from the chair and gestured him out of the room.

As he followed her to the living room he knew he was going to have to tell her something. He couldn't afford to alienate her until Jack contacted him and yet he had to be wary of telling her so much that she wound up in danger.

A slippery slope, he thought as he sat on the sofa and she eased into the chair across from him, an expectant look on her beautiful face. She looked hot in the yellow T-shirt that clung to her full breasts and he wished he could just sit and appreciate looking at her instead of having the discussion they were about to have.

"You have to understand, if I tell you too much it could be dangerous for you," he began.

"I don't care. You owe me some explanations," she replied. "I've not only put my job on the line, but also my sense of what's right. You owe me something. Were you born with the mental telepathy? I've heard that twins sometimes share that kind of awareness with each other."

"No, we weren't born with the ability. As twins we were close, but normal. The ability came later." He'd promised he wouldn't get into her thoughts without her permission but as her eyes narrowed he wished he could see exactly what she was thinking.

"You aren't going to tell me the truth, are you?" she finally asked.

"Everything I've told you is the truth."

"But it's not the whole truth."

"I can't tell you everything." A deep weariness washed over him and reminded him that he was still not himself, still physically and mentally weak. "Willa, for the past six months you've been the most important person in my life. It was your spirit, your optimism and care, that got me through the darkness. Hopefully very soon my brother will contact me and I'll be out of your life. The last thing I want to do is give you information that, if somehow these men find you, will put you at risk. I care about you too much to do that."

Her gaze softened. "It's hard to argue with you when you use that kind of logic."

"Then don't," he replied.

"You're tired. Your color isn't good," she said briskly and stood. "Why don't you take a little nap while we wait for your brother to contact you?"

He nodded, too exhausted to argue with her. He stretched out against the sofa cushions. "What are you going to do?" he asked.

"I'm going to contact the hospital and see if anyone knows anything about your whereabouts.

It will seem suspicious if I don't. Everyone there knew you were a special project of mine." She blushed at the words and then disappeared into the kitchen.

He closed his eyes. She wasn't the only one who had considered him a special project. Despite his weariness every muscle in his body tightened as he thought of the man who had destroyed his life.

Uncle Ken, that was what he'd had the two orphaned twins call him when he'd taken custody of them after their parents' deaths in a car accident. He'd taken the grieving boys from the only home they'd known to a small house in a remote area. For the next eight years the boys were isolated from everyone except Uncle Ken, who gave them weekly injections and educated and tested them.

His muscles began to relax as he heard Willa on the phone in the next room. He shoved away those dark memories of the past and instead focused on the familiar, comforting sound of her voice.

Within minutes he was asleep and dreaming, and in his dream he stood in the dark, cold forest with his brother, free for the first time in fifteen years.

Despite the danger he knew they were in, his senses exploded, alive with sensations. The cold tickle of grass beneath his bare feet, the rustling sound of the wind through the last of the autumn leaves, the clean, sharp scent of the air, all combined to give him a heady rush.

The moment of exhilaration was shattered as the alarm of impending danger thrummed through his veins and rang in his head. *Run*. Jared didn't know if it was his own thought or Jack's, but he followed the command.

He ran with no thought to where he was going, only the need to get away. Both he and his brother were in perfect physical condition and Jared ran like a marathon man, his only desire to put as many miles as possible between himself and the place where he'd been held.

In his dream his heart pumped and his legs worked to carry him farther and farther away. Freedom sang through him with each mile he traveled.

They were going to do it. They were finally going to get away, to be free. Success filled him as his legs continued to pump.

And then he was crossing a highway and headlights appeared from nowhere and he saw the car and knew he was about to be hit. Then pain—excruciating pain.

"Jared, it's okay. You're having a nightmare." Willa's voice cut through the intense pain, her slender hand cool on his forehead as he jerked awake.

With a ragged breath he sat up. "Sorry," he said as she stepped away from the sofa.

"No need to apologize. Want to talk about it?"

He smiled, as always touched by her concern for him. "It was just a bad dream." He ran his hand through his hair. "I remember a man gave me a ride in a big truck for a while and then I got out and was walking along the side of the road. I was hit by a car. Do you know who hit me?" he asked.

She shook her head. "According to the police officer who accompanied you into the hospital it was a hit-and-run. A couple from another car saw it happen and thought the driver might be drunk. They called for help and stayed with you until the ambulance and police arrived. Is that what you were dreaming about?"

"Yeah, the accident. How long was I asleep?"

"About an hour. I made you some soup if you feel like you could eat."

"Yeah, I am hungry." He got up from the sofa and stretched to unkink his muscles, aware of her gaze sliding across the width of his shoulders, down the length of his legs, before she quickly looked away.

"Jared, last night before I went to the hospital…" She broke off but he knew exactly what she was talking about. "I had a crazy dream." She met his gaze and he didn't have to read her mind to know what she was asking of him.

"It was a beautiful dream," he said.

Her eyes widened. "Was it real?"

"As real as a dream can be," he replied. A wave of sadness swept through him as he realized the dream of Willa was all he'd have to take away from his time with her.

WILLA SET THE BOWL of soup in front of him and then sat in the chair opposite him at the table. She still wasn't sure what to think about him, but she believed he was in some kind of trouble. She didn't understand it, found his most simple explanation cryptic and even questioned the reality of a twin brother.

She had no idea what kind of brain damage he might have suffered because of the accident that had put him in her hospital, had no idea if what was going on now was a result of his brain not functioning on all cylinders.

There was no question that he could read her thoughts, that somehow he was able to communicate with her in her mind.

"I didn't realize how hungry I was," he said, breaking in to her thoughts.

"An appetite is a good sign." She got up to get the saucepan to refill his bowl. As she stood close to him she caught the scent of him, a clean male coupled with a hint of something wild. She focused her attention on filling the bowl and tried not to think about the hot dream they had shared.

"Tell me about Paul," he said.

She nearly dropped the saucepan in his lap. "How do you know about him?" she asked as she carried the pan back to the stove burner.

His electric-blue eyes held her gaze. "All I really know is that you thought about him a lot over the past six months and when you did, you were sad."

She returned to her chair. "It definitely isn't fair, this gift of yours," she exclaimed. "You know way too much about me and I don't know anything about you."

"Paul was your lover?" he asked, obviously ignoring her comments. He placed his spoon down on the table and looked at her with a single-minded intent.

She leaned back and worried a hand through her hair. "Paul Callahan was my high-school sweetheart, the only man I really dated and the one I thought I was going to marry. About eighteen months ago he broke up with me. He told me he wanted to see what was out there, date other women and explore new experiences."

"He hurt you," Jared said.

She sighed. "For months after it happened, I was devastated. He'd given me no warning signs, no clue that he was unhappy, that he wanted anything different than me. The breakup was particularly hard because we shared the same friends, hung out in the same places. I finally decided I needed a fresh start in another city, a place to make new friends and build a new life, so I moved here from Kansas City."

"Your Paul was a fool," he said with conviction.

She laughed, surprised to discover that thoughts of Paul no longer hurt. "I like to think so," she agreed. "Actually, I suppose I should be grateful to him that he decided he wanted out before we got married. A breakup is definitely easier than a divorce. What about you, any old lovers running around in your past?"

The spark of light in his eyes was instantly doused and he picked up his spoon once again. "No, nothing like that," he replied.

She was twenty-six years old and she guessed him to be at least her age, perhaps a year or two older. She wanted to press him on the subject. Surely there had been some woman in his life who had meant something special to him, but there was a darkness in his eyes, a knotted muscle in his jaw, that let her know the subject was closed.

"I called the hospital while you were asleep. The consensus is that you awoke from the coma and were disoriented and wandered off. They've contacted the local authorities, hoping that somebody will find you and return you to the hospital."

"Did they mention if anyone else had been by to see me?"

"I asked," she replied. "And the answer was no, nobody else has made any inquiries about you."

"That's because they already know I'm gone." He frowned and stared down into his soup bowl. "I hope nobody saw us leaving together last night."

"I think if anyone would have seen us, we'd already know by now." Despite the fact that she had no idea who was after him and what they might want, a small chill stole through her.

He finished the soup and she carried the bowl to the sink, where she rinsed it and placed it in the dishwasher. "You have no family?" he asked.

"My mother died five years ago after a long battle with cancer." She leaned with her back against the cabinet, reluctant to return to the table where the scent of him made her remember the wild and wonderful dream they'd shared.

"It was during her illness that I decided I wanted to become a nurse," she continued. "My father walked out on the two of us when I was four years old. I really don't have any memories of him. So, no, I don't have any family." She'd once believed that Paul would be her family, that together they would have children and build a life filled with love and laughter.

Jared got up from the table and approached where she stood. "One of the strongest emotions I felt from you, one of the thoughts that was uppermost in your mind, was your loneliness."

He stopped just in front of her, so close she only had to lean forward a little bit to touch him. Her mouth went ridiculously dry at his nearness. "I just haven't taken the time to make too many friends here." A nervous laugh escaped her. "You must never get lonely. I mean, anytime you feel that way you can just jump into somebody's mind."

"You'd be surprised at how unpleasant being in somebody else's mind can be," he replied. "But I never found it unpleasant to be in yours."

He reached out and touched a strand of her hair that had escaped from the ponytail holder at the nape of her neck. Her breath caught in her throat. "So soft," he murmured more to himself than to her. "I knew it would feel that way."

Her heart slammed a quickened rhythm in her chest as he took a step closer to her, his fingers still entwined in her lock of hair.

At that moment her cell phone rang. She jumped away from him and he dropped his hand to his side. "Maybe that's Jack," he said, hope or some other emotion she was afraid to identify thick in his voice.

She pulled her cell phone from her pocket and answered, but it wasn't Jack. It was Nancy from the hospital calling to chat about the gossip making the rounds with John Doe's disappearance.

Jared returned to the living room and Willa remained in the kitchen. As she talked to her friend she tried to ignore the sizzle of heat Jared's touch had created inside her.

What was it about Jared that affected her so viscerally? She'd like to believe it was just because of the dream, because he'd invaded her sleep and created intimate visions that had not only stirred her physically, but had also been a balm to her loneliness.

But she knew it was more than that. The truth was that throughout the past six months Jared had been in her care she'd felt a special connection with him.

She also realized now that the comforting voice she'd often heard inside her head, the voice she'd assumed might be a figment of her own imagination or a deep-seated memory of her father's, had actually been Jared's.

Nancy had no news to impart and it didn't take the two long to finish their conversation. It was Saturday morning and Willa wasn't scheduled to be back at the hospital until Monday morning. By that time she knew Jared planned on being gone.

It was ridiculous that she found this particular thought depressing. He meant nothing to her and as his nurse she was only glad that he'd survived his coma and come out on the other side relatively unscathed.

Whatever was going on in his life, whatever his

future held, it had nothing to do with her and she'd do well to remember that.

Still, aside from the fact that he had mental telepathy, there was something a bit off about him. When he'd touched her hair there had been a strange look of awe on his face, as if it was the first time he'd ever touched a woman's hair.

Crazy, a man who looked like Jared had to have had women in his life unless he'd been living under a mushroom, she thought dryly.

She left the kitchen and found him staring out her window into her backyard. "Your flowers are beautiful," he said. "Do they smell as pretty as they look?"

"You don't know what flowers smell like?" she asked in surprise.

He turned to face her but his eyes didn't quite meet hers. "I guess maybe the coma messed with some of my memories. I just don't remember what they smell like."

"Jared, even if you don't go back to my hospital, wherever you end up you really should check yourself in and have some tests run. We can't know what results the coma might have left you with, what problems you might have that need to be medically addressed."

"I'm fine," he replied and began to pace the length of the floor like a restless tiger. "I just need to hear from Jack." There was an edgy frustration in his voice.

"What happens if your brother doesn't contact you?"

He stopped pacing and stood perfectly still, his features taut with tension. "Then I'll have to make other plans. All I really know is that I need to get as far away from here as quickly as possible." He offered her a smile that didn't quite reach his eyes. "Don't you worry about it. I'll figure out something."

She knew he meant to assure her but when the next two hours passed without a call from his brother, she wondered what possible plans he could make. He had no identification, no money and no car.

It's not your problem, a little voice whispered in her head. She looked at him sharply, wondering if it was his voice, but he'd turned back to face the window and she realized the voice wasn't his, but rather her own.

But it wasn't true. Since the moment she'd helped him leave the hospital his problems had become her own. Wasn't there some sort of Chinese proverb about if you saved somebody's life then you were responsible for that life forever?

She felt responsible for him. The idea of him walking out her door without the means to take care of himself appalled her.

When her phone rang again she wasn't sure who jumped more, her or Jared. He whirled around to face her as she pulled the phone from her pocket; the tension that wafted from him was palpable in the air.

The caller ID read *unknown caller* and she opened the phone and breathed a tentative hello. "You visited a Web site?" The deep voice sounded a lot like Jared's. "Who are you?" he asked.

"A friend," she replied. "I have somebody here who would like to speak to you." She held out the phone to Jared.

He took the phone and raised it to his ear. He said nothing for a moment and then sighed in obvious relief. "Thank God," he said into the receiver and then spoke Willa's address. "Yes, I understand. I'll be waiting."

He hung up and joy filled his eyes, a joy that warmed his features and made him even more attractive. "That was Jack. He's alive and well and he's sending somebody to get me."

"I'm so glad, Jared," she said. "Did he say when that somebody would be here?"

"Jack said by nightfall. He didn't tell me where he was or who was coming. He just told me that the man who came for me would mention that seashells are cool to collect."

"What's with all the beach references?" she

asked, remembering that the note he'd had her send to the Web site had mentioned birthday parties at the beach.

He smiled and once again she was struck by his handsomeness. "Jack and I share only one real strong memory of our parents. For our fourth birthday they took us to the beach. I can still remember the feel of the warm sand beneath my feet, the scent of the salt water and the laughter we all shared that day. I think it was the last time Jack and I were truly happy."

Willa looked at him in stunned surprise. "Surely you've been happy since then."

"If I was, then I can't remember it." Once again a smile curved his sensual lips. "But everything is going to be okay now. Within the next few hours I'll be reunited with Jack and everything will be fine."

"Wait here, I'll be right back," Willa said. She hurried down the hallway and into her bedroom, where she opened the drawer that held her underwear. She found the black lacy bra that she rarely wore and inside one of the cups was the stash of emergency fund money that had been left after she'd bought his clothes.

She grabbed the wad of folded bills and carried it with her back into the living room, where Jared remained standing where she'd left him.

"Jared, I want you to take this." She held out the

money. "There's almost seven hundred dollars here. I want you to take it in case something happens."

He reached out but instead of taking the money from her he folded her fingers over it. "Put your money away, Willa. I won't take any more from you than I already have."

He released her hand but the softness in his eyes held her rooted in place.

"Are you sure?" she asked. "I don't mind. You're probably going to need it more than I will."

"Positive."

She stuffed the bills into her back pocket and started to walk away, but he grabbed her arm and pulled her close to him. Her heartbeat crashed through her like rumbling thunder.

"There is one last thing you can do for me, Willa." His voice was slightly husky and a rivulet of warmth began in her toes and swept up through her body.

"What's that?" she asked and heard the tremor of anticipation in her voice.

"Kiss me."

Before she could reply his arms tightened around her and pulled her closer and his mouth descended to hers. Tentative at first, his lips whispered against hers as if tasting something new and different.

It took only a moment for his tongue to lightly touch her lower lip, as if seeking permission to deepen the kiss. She opened her mouth to him and used her tongue to welcome him, overwhelmed by the desire that the kiss evoked.

She wouldn't have thought it possible, but it was better than her dream and she wanted the kiss to go on forever.

The window nearest them crashed inward and the kiss was ended with his gasp and her outcry. A large cylindrical object lay on the floor, hissing smoke that quickly filled the room and burned Willa's eyes and the back of her throat.

The smoke grew so thick so fast she lost sight of Jared and cried out his name in fear. She felt his hand grab hers as her head spun and a fierce dizziness gripped her. He tried to pull her toward the door but they both careened sideways with disorientation.

She had no time to wonder what was happening or who was responsible. She only had a moment to recognize that whoever was after Jared had somehow found him here and now they were in deep trouble.

Willa! She heard his frantic voice calling out her name in her brain just before a profound darkness rushed up to grab her.

Chapter Four

Jared came to with a gasp and sat up. Instantly he gripped the sides of his head with his hands and squeezed his eyes more tightly closed. His head pounded with an intensity that made his stomach buck and roll with nausea.

He drew in several deep, steadying breaths, slowly lowered his hands from his head and opened his eyes. He was in a small room, the green paint on the walls chipping and faded. There was a single small and narrow window high in the wall with bars to prevent entry or exit. He had no idea where he was; the room was completely unfamiliar.

But the setup in the room was terrifyingly familiar. He was lying on a steel examination room table. Overhead was a bright lamp suspended from the ceiling. He knew from experience that there was no point trying the door, that it would be locked to keep him inside.

He lay back on the table, his head reeling with residual fogginess. Had his escape only been a fantasy? Had he dreamed of the forest with his brother and the run through the night? The accident and the coma, had they only been figments of his imagination?

No! He'd smelled the clean fresh air of a November night. He'd gripped his brother's hand as they said their farewells. The slam of the car into his body had been real. He'd felt the pain of that impact. And he'd kissed a woman with the sweetest, hottest lips.

Willa. As her name exploded in his brain his memories came rushing back. The kiss, the shatter of glass, the noxious gas that had filled the room— his heart slammed against his ribs as the memories exploded in his head.

They'd found them. The escape from the hospital had all been for nothing. Somehow Uncle Ken and his men had discovered that he was at Willa's. What had they done with her?

He closed his eyes and concentrated. *Willa.* Mentally he reached out for her. He called her name several times and then listened deep inside his brain, in the place he'd never understood, in the place where his ability lived.

Nothing. He couldn't pick up any of her thoughts. She was either dead or still unconscious. A wave of grief suffused him as he thought about her. He'd brought danger to her doorstep. If anything had happened to her it was all his fault.

She'd put herself and her job on the line to help him and now if she were still alive he feared it wouldn't be for long. They wouldn't want to leave any loose ends. The men who had hunted him were ruthless when it came to protecting themselves and their operation. Willa would simply be collateral damage in their eyes.

Jared strained once again in an effort to communicate with Willa and when he was unsuccessful he tried to make contact with Jack. Again he failed. Finally in desperation he tried to pick up the thoughts of anyone who might be near.

Nothing. He didn't know if perhaps the gas that he'd inhaled had affected his ability to read minds or if somehow the people who held him were successfully blocking his attempts.

Where was he? Were they even still in Grand Forks? He studied the light at the small window and decided it was dusk. That meant that well over eight hours had passed since the gas had overcome him. He could have been transported almost anywhere in the world in that length of time.

He steeled himself as he heard the sound of heavy footsteps outside the door. He got up off the table, pleased that his headache had begun to ebb.

Maybe he could overtake whoever walked in.

Although he had nowhere near the strength he once did, his brief time at Willa's had brought some of it back.

He tensed as he heard a key turn in the lock, then it swung open and a tall, broad-shouldered bald man entered, his blue eyes glittering as he leveled a gun at Jared's stomach.

The faint scar at the edge of one eyelid let Jared know the identity of the man. Blue. The man was one of the triplets Jared had only known as Red, Blue and Green.

"Back up," he said.

There was no way Jared could do anything but comply. He was no match for a bullet, no matter how much of his strength had returned.

As Jared backed away, another man entered the room and Jared's blood ran cold. Uncle Ken. Kenneth Sykes wasn't a big man. He stood about five foot nine, but his slight frame and stooped shoulders made him appear shorter, smaller.

Although he was only sixty years old his hair was snow-white and hung in thin and wiry strands almost to his shoulders. In his white lab coat he looked like a harmless absent-minded professor until you gazed into his eyes. In the depths of his brown eyes resided a cunning, intelligent monster.

"Ah, Jared, my boy, I can't tell you how happy I am to see you again," Kenneth said.

"Where's Willa?" Jared asked. "I demand you take me to her immediately."

Kenneth laughed, although the sound had nothing to do with any happiness or joy. "I'm afraid you're in no position to issue demands," he replied.

He closed the door and returned his gaze to Jared. "You don't look too bad considering what you've been through. From what I heard it's a miracle you survived the car accident."

Jared remained silent and tried to probe Kenneth's thoughts, hoping to find out something about Willa's condition. But the man had always been good at blocking Jared.

"Did you really think I was just going to let you go? After all the time and all the money I've invested in you and your brother?" Kenneth shook his head, a gesture that sent his hair flying around his face. "Foolish boy. And it won't be long before we have Jack back where he belongs, as well."

A surge of hope soared through Jared. They hadn't caught Jack. He was still out there someplace and Jared knew his brother would do everything in his power to help Jared.

"I must admit, it took us far longer than I'd initially thought to find you," Kenneth continued. He was a man who had always loved the sound of his own voice. "It took us months before we finally began to check the hospitals and morgues to see if you might have ended up there. Do you have any idea how many John Does wind up hospitalized or dead?"

"Where is this place?" Jared asked. He knew they weren't in the place he remembered, the place where fifteen years of his life had been lost to isolation and experimentation.

"Unfortunately with you and your brother's escape we had to abandon our previous accommodations." He gestured around the room. "This is merely temporary until our funding allows us to move our project overseas."

Jared had hoped that by keeping Kenneth talking Blue would relax his stance, allow the gun to drift away from Jared, but the man remained on alert, the weapon never wavering an inch from its target.

"I see one thing that hasn't changed is that you still have the Three Stooges working for you," Jared said and nodded toward Blue.

"There have been several changes since we last spoke," Kenneth continued. "Sadly, the triplets are now twins. Red sacrificed his life for our cause."

Jared looked at Blue, seeking a glimmer of grief, a spasm of pain created by the mention of his brother's death, but there was nothing. Blue and his brothers had been conditioned to care about nothing and nobody. Their sole job was to protect and serve Kenneth.

"What do you want?" Jared finally asked.

"I want samples from you—tissue and blood," Kenneth replied.

"Are you asking my permission?" Jared stared at the man he hated more than anyone else on the face of the earth. "Why not just drug me and take what you want?"

Kenneth frowned in obvious irritation. "Because I don't want my results to be tainted with any drugs that might be in your system."

"And what makes you think I'd cooperate?" Jared asked.

A small smile curved Kenneth's lips. "Because Willa is in another room and I'm sure you wouldn't want to be responsible for her death."

Jared's heart thrummed an unnatural rhythm. He'd halfway hoped that they'd left her lying on the floor in her living room. "She doesn't really mean anything to me, but I don't want to see her hurt. How do I know she isn't already dead?"

"I guess you'll just have to trust me. But if you choose not to cooperate then I'll have her brought in here and you can watch while Blue slits her throat," Kenneth said, his voice holding no more emotion than if he were discussing the weather.

For just a brief moment Jared picked up a thought inside Blue's head. It was unadulterated glee at the prospect of a kill. In that thought Jared knew that at least for the moment Willa was still alive.

"She doesn't know anything," Jared said. "I didn't tell her anything about you or about me or about what you've been doing. She's innocent in all of this. Just let her go and she won't make any problems for you."

"A touching display of emotion from a man who professes not to care," Kenneth replied, "but all I want to know is if you intend to cooperate."

"Okay, damn you, I'll cooperate," Jared exclaimed. He knew without a doubt that refusing to allow Kenneth to take his samples would result in Willa's death. He would cooperate for now and hope that somehow, some way, he could get them both out of here.

"I knew you'd see things my way," Kenneth said and motioned Jared to the examining table.

Reluctantly Jared lay back on the table and as Kenneth strapped Jared's wrists down with thick leather bands, he motioned to Blue.

Blue opened the door and a man Jared had never seen before entered. He was clad in a lab coat and pushed a metal stand holding a variety of instruments.

Jared's heart thudded with anxiety. There was no way what he was about to endure would be pleasant, but if it kept Willa alive for even another moment then it was worth it.

"Thank you, George," Kenneth said to the man. "That will be all." The man gave a curt nod and left the room.

"Before I begin with the samples, there's something else I need to do." Kenneth picked up a large syringe and advanced toward Jared.

"What is that?" Jared asked, a new alarm screeching through him.

"It's just a little enhancement, nothing for you to worry about." Kenneth stabbed the needle into Jared's upper arm and pressed the plunger. Jared felt the liquid as it burned from the injection site through his entire body and he wondered what new hell Kenneth was visiting on him.

"And now, for the samples," Kenneth said.

A new dizziness struck Jared and he fought against it. "Damn you," he said as Kenneth began to take blood samples.

Kenneth chuckled. "Now is that any way to talk to the man who raised you? The man who clothed and fed you for the past twenty-three years? Just relax, Jared. I'm afraid that withdrawing a bit of muscle matter will be painful."

As Kenneth leaned over him, Jared saw the flash of silver just above the pocket in his lab coat. An instrument of some kind, he thought. As Kenneth moved closer to him, despite Jared's bound wrist, he managed to pluck it from Kenneth's pocket.

A scalpel!

Jared heart pounded as he carefully closed his

fingers around it in an attempt to hide it. There was no way he could use it now, with his arms tied down, but perhaps it would come in handy later…if there was a later.

Before he could put together another rational thought the pain of Kenneth's sampling, combined with the dizziness, made Jared fall unconscious.

WILLA!

The voice sliced through the darkness of Willa's dreams. *Go away,* she thought. *It's my day off. I just want to sleep a little while longer.*

Willa, are you there? You must wake up.

The voice was an irritating roar in her brain that refused to be quiet. As it yelled again she came to consciousness.

She opened her eyes and found herself on a cot in a room she'd never seen before. Her head throbbed with the worst headache she'd ever had in her life and she closed her eyes again as her brain worked to make sense of things.

Willa, are you there?

Jared! His name exploded in her mind and she suddenly remembered the crash of glass, the burning in the back of her throat and the gas that had knocked them unconscious.

Despite the pain in her head she sat up. "I'm here, Jared. Can you hear me?" She concentrated as hard as she could, hoping that the voice she heard in her head was truly his and not her imagination.

Where are you?

"I don't know. I'm in a room," she whispered.

Describe it to me.

"It's a small room with peeling ugly green paint and a small window with bars. There's a door with a viewing slat in it." She swung her feet over the edge of the cot and sat up. "Where are you?"

Someplace close, I think. Look carefully around the room. Tell me what else you see.

She looked around again. *Mouse droppings in the corner. Cobwebs everywhere.*

She realized she'd stopped speaking aloud and was communicating with him only through her thoughts. She might have been awed by the feat if she wasn't so terrified. *There's a grate in the ceiling. Part of the ventilation system, I think.* She heard the sound of footsteps approaching. *Somebody's coming!*

She quickly lay back on the cot and closed her eyes as fear screamed inside her. She heard the door swing open and there was a long moment of silence.

"I know you're awake," a deep voice finally said. "You can pretend to still be out cold, but I can hear your heart beating like a trapped rabbit. Come on, Ms. Tyler. You're wasting my time."

Willa opened her eyes and sat up. The man

standing just inside the door looked kind of like pictures she'd seen of Albert Einstein. He looked fairly benign, but the bald man standing just behind him looked like a mountain with a gun.

"Who are you and how do you know my name?" she asked the older man.

"It doesn't matter who I am and your coworkers at the hospital were more than happy to talk about you with me. Of course I had to be careful in asking questions, I didn't want to draw attention to myself. After Jared disappeared from the hospital everyone was talking about you and how disappointed you would be because Jared had become your special project."

"Where's Jared? What have you done with him?" She tried to keep the fear out of her voice.

"He's alive. I need to keep him alive for the next couple of days." He took a step closer to her and Willa fought the impulse to shrink back from him. If it were just the two of them in the room she would have tried to fight him in an attempt to escape, but the presence of the bald man with the gun shot that idea right out of her head.

"Unfortunately the two of you have become a liability," the older man continued. "I'm thinking a murder-suicide scenario."

Her heart seemed to skip a beat. "What are you talking about?"

"I need Jared for a few more days, but after that the two of you become useless. My friend Blue—" he gestured to the man behind him "—will shoot Jared and then we'll shoot you and make it look like a suicide. You were obsessed with your patient and they'll believe that when he woke up and didn't want anything to do with you, you went crazy. You took him from the hospital and killed him and then killed yourself."

"You're insane," she exclaimed. "Nobody will ever believe that."

"Don't be so sure. People love to believe the worst of others and think of all the juicy gossip the story will provoke in the hospital." The man's brown eyes hardened. "He shouldn't have involved you in this. You stepped into business that wasn't your own." He backed up toward the door. "What did he tell you about himself? About his ability?"

"His ability? What are you talking about?" She hoped her voice and her features betrayed nothing. "He was delusional, said somebody was after him. I decided to play along with his delusion and got him out of the hospital, but the minute we got to my place he collapsed on my sofa and didn't say much of anything. Would you please just tell me what's going on?"

The man studied her, his brown eyes seeming to attempt to peer into her very brain. "You made a fatal mistake in involving yourself with Jared. I just wanted to let you know that you should enjoy your last few days as my guest."

The minute the two men stepped out the door a deep sob ripped through Willa. She'd known they were in trouble, but she hadn't processed just how desperate their situation was until now.

Even though she knew that tears wouldn't help, she couldn't stop the sobs that continued to escape her. They were going to die.

She would never know true love, she'd never have the babies she'd once dreamed of having. Jared would never get the opportunity to reunite with his brother.

She still didn't understand what was going on, who the men were and what Jared had been through in his past. But even knowing what she did now she would have still helped Jared get away from the hospital.

"Jared." She whispered his name and concentrated. *I'm here.*

The sound of his voice inside her head chased away the last of her tears and somehow comforted her.

They're going to kill us.

Not if we can escape, his voice thundered in her brain. *You said there was a grate in the ceiling. Can you reach it?*

Willa looked up at the white grate overhead.

Maybe if she moved the cot beneath it and stood on it and jumped she could reach it. But then what?

It should lead you into a ventilation system. You can use it to find me.

And then what? she thought again.

And then we'll figure something out. At least we'll have some time together.

She wasn't sure he intended for her to pick up on that last thought. She eyed the grate again. It seemed like a hopeless idea, but she couldn't just sit here and do nothing. She had to at least try to save her own life, to save Jared's.

She moved the cot beneath the grate and stood on it. On her tiptoes her fingers could touch the cool metal. But she could see the four screws that held it in place. What was she supposed to do about them?

Her brain whirled. This place was old—really old. Maybe she could pull it down despite the screws. She reached up and grabbed it with her fingers and pulled.

Nothing.

She dropped her arms with a grunt of frustration. Drawing a deep breath, she tried again and this time she felt it give. She pulled harder and gasped with success as the Sheetrock holding the screws gave way and the grate pulled loose.

I did it! The grate is off!

Good girl. Now, see if you can get into the vent.

Willa eyed the hole in the ceiling. Because of her work as a nurse, she had upper-body strength from lifting patients, but she didn't know if she was capable of lifting herself up and into the hole.

"You won't know until you try," she muttered aloud. The first two attempts were failures. Sheetrock crumbled beneath her fingers as she tried to find purchase.

The third time, with muscles trembling from the strain, she managed to pull herself up and into the vent. For a moment she remained unmoving as she tried to catch her breath. *I'm in,* she finally managed to think. She lay on her belly and tried not to feel claustrophobic.

The vent was long and dark in both directions with only occasional faint glows of light coming in from other grates.

I don't know which direction to go.

Just move and hopefully I'll be able to tell if you're getting farther away from me or closer.

Scared out of her wits, worried that at any moment she might fall through the ceiling, Willa began to crawl her way down the length of the vent.

Willa, talk to me. I need to hear you so I know if you're getting closer or not.

I'm just praying that I don't fall into the ceiling and that I don't make a noise that will alert some-

body as to where I am. She approached a grate where light shone upward and she peered down. It was an empty room, much like the one where she had been held.

I just passed an empty room, she thought. *I just hope nobody realizes I'm gone from my room. The bald man with the gun was so scary.* She allowed her thoughts to continue as she crawled through the narrow vent.

There was no way that this would be a viable escape plan for Jared. Even though he was thin, his shoulders were far too wide to be able to maneuver the narrow space.

She passed another room, also empty, and tried not to think about what their next move might possibly be.

I think you're getting closer. His thought held a tremor of excitement and a mirrored emotion rushed through Willa.

She crawled faster as she saw another grate. When she reached it she peered down and gasped as she saw Jared on an examining table. *Jared, I'm right above you.*

He looked up toward the grate and she could see the glitter of his blue eyes. She pushed the grate, trying to dislodge it on one side and then catch it before it could clatter to the floor.

Her heart thudded frantically as she worked and

finally managed to get it off and in her hands. She angled it up into the vent and placed it next to her, then dangled down from the hole and dropped to the floor.

Instantly she rushed to Jared's side and fought the tears that once again threatened to erupt. "Unstrap my wrists," he said.

Tears blurred her vision as she quickly unfastened the straps and he got up from the table. He pulled her up against him and she buried her face in his shirt.

"I'm sorry, Willa. I'm so sorry I got you into this," he murmured against her hair.

"It's okay," she said and reluctantly stepped out of his embrace. "I just hope you have a plan."

"I do." He opened his hand and she saw a scalpel.

"How did you get it?" It was then she saw the evidence of what they'd done to him. The crook of his right arm was bloody and held puncture wounds. A piece of his skin had been cut away on his upper arm, leaving a bloody, oozing sore. "Oh, Jared," she exclaimed.

He grabbed her by the shoulders and forced her to look into his face. "It's okay. I'm fine. We need to move fast."

He quickly told her his plan and the fear that had momentarily been held at bay while she'd stood in his arms returned tenfold.

It was a risky plan, one that would either

succeed or see them both dead. But she knew that if they did nothing they'd be dead anyway.

Jared got back on the examination-room table and Willa arranged the straps across his wrists so that it looked as though he was still bound. She then took a position against the wall that would place her behind the door when it opened.

Ready?

She nodded as all of her muscles tensed and fear screamed inside her head.

"Blue!" Jared yelled, his voice filled with agony. "Blue, get in here!"

As the door opened, Willa held her breath.

"What the hell do you want?" Blue asked from the doorway.

Jared lifted his head and his features were twisted in agony. "You've got to help me. Burning. I'm burning up inside." He dropped his head back, as if he were too weak to hold it up.

Blue took three steps toward him, bringing him into Willa's view. *Now!* Jared's voice yelled in her head and she threw herself toward Blue and pushed him as hard as she could in Jared's direction.

Jared sprang up off the table and stabbed the scalpel into Blue's stomach. Blue careened backward and hit the floor, his head smacking it with a sickening thud. He didn't move again.

"Come on." Jared grabbed Willa's hand and

pulled her to the door. He peered outside into the hallway and then tugged her along.

They raced down the empty hall, stopping only at each room they came to so Jared could peer inside. An old institute of some kind, Willa thought as they passed room after room.

Twice they heard the sound of voices drawing closer and shot into one of the empty rooms to wait until the threat had passed.

Moment by moment, footstep by footstep, they made their way silently through a maze of corridors and rooms until finally they reached an exit door that led to the outside.

Willa blinked and waited for her eyes to adjust to the twilight shadows that had descended. As Jared gripped her hand more tightly they took off running toward a wooded area in the distance.

With each step Willa expected to hear the sound of a yell of alarm or the explosion of a gunshot, but there was nothing. They reached the woods and as they paused to catch their breath Willa looked back at the building where they had been held.

"I know this place," she said in surprise. She turned and looked at Jared. "It used to be a psychiatric hospital but it was closed down years ago. I know where we are."

"Where?"

"On the south side of Grand Forks."

He grabbed her arm. "Come on, we have to keep moving. Sooner or later somebody is going to know that we're gone and they'll come searching for us."

They moved deeper and deeper into the woods. Jared would stop every few minutes and cock his head to listen and then they'd continue on.

They didn't speak, either verbally or nonverbally. Willa's only thoughts were of escape, of putting as much distance as possible between them and their captors.

They had been half walking, half running for about an hour when Willa tripped over a thick root and stumbled to the ground.

"Wait, I have to stop," she exclaimed as she dropped to a sitting position and rubbed her knee. "I need to catch my breath."

Jared stood perfectly still, his eyes cast in the distance. He looked down at her with alarm in his eyes. "We don't have time to rest. They know we're gone," he said. "And the hunt has begun."

Chapter Five

Night fell hard in the woods. One minute there was light and the next there was almost none. Willa was afraid—of the dark, of the men chasing them and of all the strange sounds the woods offered in the darkness of night. Jared tried to comfort her with reassuring thoughts but he wasn't sure how much it helped.

He held tight to her hand, trying to maneuver around trees and through brush with only the filtered moonlight to aid them.

Twice he picked up on the thoughts of the men Kenneth had sent into the woods to find them. He pulled Willa against him and stood still until the voices in his head grew faint once again and he knew the men had moved away and he and Willa were safe to continue.

They finally burst out of the woods and into a quiet residential neighborhood and paused to catch their breath. A dog barked in the distance and a big white cat streaked across the street, but there was nothing else to make Jared nervous.

For the past hour Jared hadn't shared his thoughts with Willa because they were a jumble of chaos. He had no idea where they were going, had no real assurances to offer her.

They couldn't go back to her house and he had no idea where they could hole up long enough for his brother to find them once again. He hadn't even been able to contact Jack through their mental telepathy.

One thing was certain, he didn't want to leave town. The last place Jack had known Jared to be had been at Willa's, and he didn't want to get too far away from that general area. He hoped that Jack was looking for them now, that whoever was supposed to meet them at Willa's would have seen the broken front window and known something had happened.

He and Willa continued to walk and finally came to rest behind a convenience store. They crouched down by a Dumpster and Jared released a weary sigh. "I think we're safe for now," he said. "I'm not picking up anything and there's no way they could have known which way we ran when we hit the woods."

"So, what now?" She winced. "I seem to be asking that a lot since I met you."

He'd dreaded her asking that question because he had no answers. An incredible guilt weighed heavy in his heart. He'd gotten her into this mess and he didn't know how to get her out.

"I don't know," he admitted. "We can't go back to your house. That's probably one of the first places they'll look. And we have no money to go anywhere else."

She stared at him for a long moment, her gray-green eyes huge in the faint glow from the convenience-store lights. "Money." She sat up and slapped her back pocket. "I have money." She reached into her pocket and pulled out the wad of bills she'd offered him what seemed like a hundred years ago, but had only been the night before.

He closed his eyes, for a moment overwhelmed with gratitude. At least with some cash they could find a place to stay and get something to eat. They could rest and get prepared for whatever might come next.

"A motel," she said as if reading his mind.

He frowned thoughtfully. Would they check the motels? Maybe eventually, but Kenneth and his cohorts had no idea that he and Willa had any cash. He figured the first place they'd look for them would be among Willa's coworkers and friends. They would check her bank accounts and credit cards for activity. That would all take some time.

Hopefully by the time Kenneth's men decided

to check all the local motels Jack would have found him and Willa and they'd be gone.

"Yes, a motel," he finally agreed. He got to his feet and helped her up. "We'll have you check in alone," he said as they continued walking down the street. "Try to do as little as possible to draw any unwanted attention. I'm hoping we'll have twenty-four to forty-eight hours before Kenneth and his men will begin checking motels."

It was almost ten when they finally stopped in front of a motel, where Jared thought they would be safe at least for the remainder of the night.

As Willa went into the lobby to check in, Jared hid in the shadows of the parking lot. He not only tried to listen to see if he could pick up any thoughts of Kenneth and his men, but also if he could pick up anything from Jack.

He could pick up a thousand thoughts from the people who were nearby—a woman was thinking that her husband was cheating on her, a man was worried about losing his job and somewhere a little girl was thinking about a little boy named David. But there was nothing from Jack and thankfully nothing from Kenneth or Blue.

He looked around the area, glad to see that there were several fast-food places nearby and a discount store on the opposite corner. This was as good a place as any to hole up.

His thoughts returned to his brother. He and Jack had never had the opportunity to test how distance would affect their mental telepathy. When they'd been locked in The Facility they had been close enough to each other that the mental communication had been easy. But he didn't know now if it was their distance from each other making it difficult or a residual effect of the coma he'd been in.

Willa returned with a room key. "I checked in to a single with a double bed. I didn't want to ask for two beds because I thought it would look suspicious. I also wrote down on a form that I'm driving a navy-blue Ford Escort. We're in unit 100 and I paid for two nights."

The room was located at the end of a long string of units. The minute they entered their room Jared checked the bathroom to see if there was a window that could be used as an escape route.

It was what he assumed a typical motel room was like—a double bed covered in a gold spread, a small round table shoved into one corner with two straight-backed chairs and a nightstand with a lamp and a clock. A television sat on top of a chest of drawers.

"Let me take a look at your shoulder," Willa said as he sat on the edge of the bed. "It looks bad." As she leaned over him to inspect his wound, he noticed the long length of her lashes, the sweet curve of her jawline, and once again he was struck with a killing guilt and a faint simmer of desire.

"I'm fine," he said and stood abruptly. He took a couple of steps away from her and she sat on the edge of the bed and gazed at him somberly.

"What did they do to you, Jared? What made that wound? And all those needle marks?" Her eyes were filled with pain for him.

"He wanted samples—blood, tissue and skin."

"The man with the long white hair?" she asked, and Jared nodded. "Who is he?"

"Why don't we call it a night and talk about it tomorrow?" he asked, still unsure how much he was willing to share with her. He held out hope that if she didn't know too much, then Kenneth would leave her alone.

"I don't think so." She crossed her arms across her chest and raised her chin in a gesture of defiance he hadn't seen before. "That man intended to kill us both. He was going to make it look like I killed you and then committed suicide. I've crawled through a heating vent and run for hours in dark scary woods to escape these people. I have a right to some answers. I need to make sense of everything that's happened."

He walked over and sat next to her on the bed. She was right. She deserved answers. "His name is

Kenneth Sykes and he's a scientist." The word tasted bitter on his lips, because he knew Sykes wasn't a true scientist, but rather a megalomaniac, a monster.

"When our parents died, somehow, I'm not sure how, he managed to get custody of me and Jack and that's when he began his experiments."

"Experiments?"

So much of what Jared knew he'd learned through his ability to read minds and Kenneth's penchant for blowing his own horn. Even thinking about it was now painful.

Willa covered one of his hands with hers, as if she sensed the pain. No wonder she was such a good nurse. She had an empathy for suffering, he thought.

He turned and looked at her. Her yellow T-shirt held streaks of dust from crawling through the heating vents. Her hair had long ago escaped its tidy tie at the nape of her neck and hung around her shoulders. She looked tired and yet her first thought was to offer him comfort. Her strength gave him his own to go back in time and tell her his story.

"Years ago Kenneth discovered that some people carried a recessive gene he called I, for Ideal. When given certain drugs the recessive genes are activated and the subjects develop heightened abilities. Jack and I had those genes and we became two of Kenneth's most successful subjects."

"Two of… You mean there are more of you?"

He nodded. "Although I don't know how many."

"Where did he get his other test subjects?" she asked.

"I don't know, but Jack and I had begun to suspect that he was kidnapping children. I heard thoughts once, the thoughts of a child missing his mother." The memory shot a shaft of pain through him. The little boy's fear had been the most difficult thing he'd ever heard.

"The bald man with the gun, who is he?" she asked.

"I don't know his real name. He was one of triplets. We only knew them as Red, Blue and Green. Kenneth told me today that Red died. Apparently he committed suicide although he didn't give me any details. It was Blue who was with Kenneth today. I think they were test subjects who didn't have the results Kenneth wanted. But they're completely devoted to Kenneth."

"Did we kill Blue?"

"I don't know," he said truthfully. "And to be honest, at this point I don't care."

"How could this happen? Where did all of this take place?" she asked incredulously.

"Initially Kenneth and Jack and I lived in a small house out in the middle of nowhere. I couldn't tell you now what state we were in or even what part of the country. Jack and I knew something wasn't right and when we were thirteen years old Jack tried to run away. Everything changed after that."

He released her hand and got up from the bed, the memories making it difficult for him to remain still. "We were taken to a new place to live. Everyone called it The Facility. It was underground, some kind of old government barracks."

He thought of the dark hallways, the small cells and the laboratory and he fought against a shiver that tried to work its way up his spine. It had been a creepy, horrible place and for fifteen years it had been his home.

He walked over to the front window and moved the curtain enough that he could peer outside to the lit parking lot. It was a quiet scene with nothing to cause him alarm. "Once we moved there I never saw Jack again although we stayed in communication through our ability. We were there for fifteen years, until the night we both escaped, the night that I was hit by the car."

"Fifteen years!" Shock made her voice slightly higher than usual. "And nobody knew? This man Sykes, who does he work for? An operation like that had to have taken tons of money."

Jared allowed the curtain to fall back across the window and turned to face Willa. "Initially Sykes and his partner, Benjamin Stewart, worked for our government, but eventually they severed all ties and took their research underground. Stewart died. I think Sykes murdered him and then the funding came from a group called the Association, factions from foreign governments who are interested in the I gene research."

He leaned with his back against the window and continued. "Kenneth told me this afternoon that he was waiting for more funding and then he was going to move the operation overseas. Somehow I've got to stop him before that happens."

"How?"

Frustration shot through him. "I don't know. Nobody is going to believe a word I say. I'm a coma patient who probably suffered brain damage. That's what everyone will think."

"But I believe you. I could corroborate your story," she protested.

He shook his head. "Once Jack finds us, you're out of this. Kenneth wants me and when he realizes we aren't together anymore, I'm hoping he'll leave you alone. I'm also hoping Jack is working on getting the operation closed down."

He was suddenly exhausted. Talking about his ordeal had been like revisiting hell. He could still remember the dank smell of The Facility, the injections and examinations he'd endured—and the aching loneliness. That had been almost as bad as anything—the isolation and loneliness that had been all-consuming.

"But you were educated." Willa's voice pulled him back from his thoughts.

He nodded. "Oh, yes, we were schooled in all subjects. Sykes wanted to create the ideal human being and we wouldn't be ideal if we were uneducated. We had access to tons of books and we were even permitted to watch television, although it didn't take me long to forego that particular treat."

"Why?" Her sober gaze held his and he saw how much she was struggling to try to understand everything about him, about his past.

"I only watched a couple of shows and they were about families—mothers and fathers raising children, children who didn't live in cells and could go outside and play. They all sat together at a table to eat their meals and they laughed together and loved each other. It was just too painful to watch what normal was and know my life was so completely abnormal."

He released a weary sigh and raked a hand through his dark hair. "I can't talk about this anymore tonight. We both should get some sleep now."

She nodded and frowned. "First thing tomorrow I'm going to the store and get medicine for your arm. You need some antibiotic cream and some bandages to cover that wound."

He offered her a tired smile. "Always the nurse. We'll worry about it in the morning," he replied. Although they both could use a shower, he stretched out on the bedspread and Willa lay next to him. When they were both settled he reached over and turned out the lamp, plunging the room in darkness.

He felt the tension in Willa's body and would have liked to read her thoughts to see what she thought of what he'd told her, what she now thought of him. But he didn't. He'd promised her he wouldn't.

He would have liked to wrap his arms around her and pull her tight against him, to feel the steady beat of her heart against his own, but he didn't do that, either.

He feared that in doing so his desire for her would rage out of control and the worst thing that could happen was that their relationship deepened to a point where telling her goodbye would not only be more difficult for him, but also for her. It was already going to be hard to tell her goodbye.

He fought against his exhaustion and reached out one last time in an effort to make contact with his brother, but there was nothing.

Where are you, Jack? he thought. *We're in trouble and we need you here.*

Willa was still tense and he knew she hadn't fallen

asleep. He wanted to reach out and comfort her, to tell her that everything was going to be all right, but the truth of the matter was he didn't know that.

What he feared most of all was that Kenneth would find them before Jack did and then all would be lost.

Chapter Six

Willa was awake long after Jared had gone to sleep. His nearness was provocative, the scent of him strangely comforting and familiar.

She wouldn't have minded if he'd put his arms around her, snuggled her close to his broad chest and stilled the lingering fear that tasted bitter in her mouth. But it was good that he slept.

She still had questions, about his life, about Kenneth Sykes and the horrible experiments that had taken place.

The whole story sounded like something out of a science-fiction magazine and yet she knew it wasn't fiction.

Kenneth Sykes had invaded her home and kidnapped her. He'd taken her to an old psychiatric lab and threatened her with death, and there was no question that Jared had a special ability. These facts alone assured her there was nothing fictitious about Jared's tale.

Her heart ached for all that Jared had been through and she was more than a little concerned about the wound on his upper arm. What if it got infected? What if the infection raged and he got sick?

With everything that was happening to them it seemed ludicrous that she should focus in on the fact that he could possibly get an infection, but it was the only thing she might be able to do something about.

How long could they hole up here? What if Jared never managed to contact his brother? What would happen when her cash ran out? Where would they go?

She finally fell asleep with the questions whirling in her head and awakened hours later to find herself alone on the bed and the sound of a shower running in the bathroom.

Sunshine seeped in around the edges of the curtains at the window. She glanced at the clock on the nightstand and was surprised to discover it was just after nine.

The water turned off in the bathroom but she didn't move from her position on the bed, as her mind continued to work overtime.

It was Sunday morning. By this time tomorrow her coworkers would be wondering what had happened to her. She never missed work. In the year that she had been an employee at the hospital she had never taken a day off.

Would she ever be able to go back to work at the hospital? Would she ever see her friends there again? The same questions that had plagued her before falling asleep were back again full force.

She turned her head as the bathroom door opened and felt her breath catch in her chest as Jared stepped out amid a puff of steam. Clad only in his low-riding jeans and with his short dark hair tousled, he looked as sexy as any man she'd ever seen.

He brought with him into the room a clean male scent that for the moment cast all her questions and concerns straight out of her head. Desire whispered through her, the desire for him to get back into the bed with her and make love.

"Good morning," he said as he raised a towel to his hair in order to finish drying it.

"Good morning," she replied, feeling suddenly ridiculously shy and on edge in a way that had nothing to do with the threat against them.

She glanced away from him, feeling the embarrassing burn of a blush washing over her cheeks. What was wrong with her? Her life had fallen apart, she had a mad scientist trying to kill her and all she could think about was how wickedly fine Jared looked half-dressed.

He looked nothing like the still, helpless patient

she'd seen for six months lying in the hospital bed. Instead he looked vital and healthy and hot.

"I thought I'd head over to the fast-food place and pick us up some breakfast," he said. "I'm starving and I'm sure you're hungry, as well."

Oh, she was hungry all right, but what she craved at the moment wouldn't be served up from any fast-food menu. "While you're gone I'll take a shower," she said. A cold shower, she thought wryly.

She pulled the cash from her back pocket and held it out to him. "Take what you need."

He hesitated a moment and then took the cash. "When we get out of this mess, I swear I'll pay you back every penny that you've spent, Willa."

She started to tell him not to worry about it, but at that moment her gaze drifted down to the wound on his upper arm and she gasped in surprise. She jumped off the bed to get a closer look.

The place where the skin had been missing was covered with a new healthy pink layer of skin. "It should have taken weeks for this kind of healing to take place," she exclaimed as her fingers ran delicately over the new flesh.

"I know. The only thing I can figure is the injection that Kenneth gave me must have contained some sort of superhealing powers," he said. "Not only is this healing miraculously fast, but I also feel better, stronger than I have in a long time."

She stepped back from him, finding his scent far too evocative. "I'm going to take a shower."

"While you do that I'll get our breakfast. Sausage or bacon?"

"Definitely bacon," she replied.

"Coffee?"

"Black."

He nodded and headed for the door as she went into the bathroom. Minutes later she stood beneath a hot stream of water and wished she had clean clothes to crawl back into.

As she washed, her mind went over all that Jared had told her the night before. A mad scientist, covert experiments—how many other test subjects had there been? Jared had mentioned the kidnapping of children. It was monstrous, utterly monstrous.

Equally as troubling was how attracted she was to the man who had once been her patient. Even now, just thinking about the way he had looked standing there in his jeans, her breasts grew heavy with a longing she'd never felt before.

It had never been this way with Paul. She'd never felt this kind of deep craving for physical intimacy with the man she'd once believed she'd marry.

She finished her shower and dried off and for a moment she remembered the kiss she'd shared with Jared just before the gas bomb had shattered her front window.

Never had Paul's kiss moved her as much and as quickly as Jared's had. With Jared it had only taken an instant for her to be so turned on that she would have tumbled right into bed with him.

For far too long her heartache over Paul had held her captive, afraid to reach out for friendship, afraid to pursue any new relationships. Now, not knowing if she would live for another week, another day, she wished she would have made different choices.

She realized that part of her intense loneliness since moving to Grand Forks had been of her own making. Several of the men working at the hospital had asked her out, but she'd declined, telling herself she wasn't ready to open her heart again.

It had been foolish to waste that time and now it was quite possible she'd run out of time. She swiped a damp cloth over her T-shirt and jeans to remove the dust that had accumulated between her crawl through the ventilation system and the run through the woods, and then finished dressing, finger-combed her damp hair as best she could and left the bathroom.

The savory scents of coffee and bacon filled the room and Jared sat in a chair at the table with two foam cups and a white paper bag in front of him.

"Breakfast is served," he said. He pulled out a couple of breakfast sandwiches, two small plastic bowls of fruit and two hash-brown patties.

"Wow, it's a feast," she said as she sat in the chair opposite his.

For the next few minutes they ate in silence. Willa finished first, pushing her hash browns toward him. She leaned back in the chair. "I still have a lot of questions about everything."

"I'll try to answer what I can." He took a sip of his coffee and then began to tackle her hash browns.

"Why can't we just go to the police?"

"Because I'm afraid Kenneth will have somebody planted in the police stations. I don't know who might be working for him. I don't even know if he's manufactured some charges against me that would get me locked up the minute I show up at a police station." He shook his head. "Right now going to the authorities is out of the question."

"The eight-pointed star Web site, is that something you and your brother set up before you escaped?"

A deep frown cut across his forehead. "No. I can't explain that. I just knew that's what I needed to look for when I got to your place. It was like it was imprinted in my brain."

Willa chewed her lower lip as she continued to look at him. "How old are you?"

"Twenty-eight. What about you?"

"Twenty-six," she replied. "How are we going to get out of this, Jared?" It was the question she'd dreaded asking because she wasn't sure he had an answer.

He finished the patty and leaned back in his chair, his gaze holding hers with a steadiness she tried to find reassuring. "I know Jack will be scouring the city looking for us. Unfortunately, I don't know where he was when he contacted me. It might take him time to get here. I'm hoping that eventually he'll get close enough that he can hear me, that I can hear him." He paused and broke eye contact with her.

"What are you not telling me?" she asked hesitantly, unsure if she really wanted to know.

"This morning while I was in the shower, I picked up on somebody's thoughts, somebody who I think is working to find us, but I don't know who he is."

"What kind of thoughts?" She wrapped her fingers around the warm coffee, an unexpected chill working up her spine.

"He was thinking about a woman named Melinda and he was worried about where we were."

"But if you could read his thoughts, then couldn't you make him hear you?" She leaned forward eagerly.

He shook his head. "I can get into his thoughts, but he doesn't seem to be able to hear me." She leaned back in frustration. "You have to understand, Willa, I don't know how my ability works. I'm not sure I've mastered the full potential and, more important, I'm not sure if this man is friend or foe. I just managed to tap in to that single thought."

"Too bad you can't just pick up the phone and call Jack."

"Even if I had a number where to reach him I wouldn't chance it. In this day and age it's relatively easy to monitor phone lines. These people have enough money and resources that by now they've probably checked your bank account and credit cards and they've probably been back into your house to see if they can find any information that might lead them to us."

"Gee, can you cheer me up any more?" she asked dryly.

He smiled sympathetically. "I'm not trying to depress you, but you have to face the reality of what we're up against."

"What about trying to contact Jack through the Web site again?" she asked. "We could go to a public library and use one of their computers."

Again he shook his head. "I can't be sure that it hasn't been compromised by now. The only thing we can do is wait and hope that Jack comes close enough that we can make contact."

The morning stretched into afternoon. Willa sat in a chair at the tiny table and turned on the television and channel-surfed, seeking news and a sense that the normal world was still out there while Jared stretched out on the bed and withdrew into himself.

He appeared to be sleeping, but she knew he was using all of his mental energy and focus to try to get in touch with his brother.

She tried to keep her gaze off him, but again and again she found herself studying him and wanting him. Washington, Adams, Jefferson, Jackson—she filled her head with the names of the presidents, afraid that he might be able to pick up on her thoughts, on her crazy desire for him.

It was just after five when he roused himself from the bed. "I'm going to get us some burgers for dinner," he said. "You want anything special?"

"No, but it worries me when you leave the room," she replied. She got up from the chair and walked over to where he stood. "I don't like you out there where something might happen to you."

He raised a hand and captured her chin between his thumb and forefinger, his blue eyes dark with an emotion she couldn't begin to identify.

"You'll know if either Jack or Kenneth comes for me. I'll make sure you know. In either case I want you to go home and live a happy life and forget all about this, all about me."

"I'm not sure Kenneth would allow that to happen," she replied.

"I'll make sure he leaves you alone. Besides, it isn't you he wants. It's me."

"You can't do that if he kills you," she protested.

"He won't. He'll want to take more samples because of the injection he gave me. As a scientist he won't want me dead before he can collect whatever he wants from me and he needs my cooperation for that. I can assure he leaves you alone by giving him my cooperation and telling him again that you know nothing about his operation and the experiments."

He dropped his hand from her chin and she fought the impulse to launch herself into his arms. How could she ever go back to her real life and forget him? He was indelibly written in her heart.

"I'll be right back," he said and with those words he left the room.

Willa moved to the window and pulled the curtain aside so she could watch him as he strode in long, quick strides across the parking lot toward the fast-food restaurant in the distance.

She dropped the curtain back into place only when he disappeared from sight. She walked over and sat on the edge of the bed and worried everything she knew around in her head.

He didn't want the authorities involved but if she didn't show up for work with no explanation she worried that one of her coworkers might go by her house and then eventually contact the police when they saw the broken window and that she wasn't there.

She looked at the telephone on the nightstand. Maybe she should call and tell them she had some issues and needed some time off. She had a week of vacation time built up, maybe now was the time to take it.

Decision made, she picked up the phone and called Nancy. It took only minutes to explain to her friend that she had some issues that required a trip back to Kansas City and that she would be taking a week of vacation time starting first thing in the morning. She apologized for the late notice and Nancy assured her it was fine and that they would look forward to her return.

Willa hung up the phone and realized her chin still burned with Jared's touch and she raised a hand and swept a finger across her lips as she remembered his kiss.

She wanted him. She wanted him more than she'd ever wanted a man in her life. And she was sure that he wanted her, too.

She'd felt his gaze lingering on her when he thought she wasn't looking, had seen a flicker of flame deep in the depths of his blue eyes. It was in his touch, it had been in his kiss. He felt desire for her just as she did for him.

Who knew how much time they had left together? It might be minutes or hours before she never saw him again. Could she say goodbye to him and never know the reality of being held in his arms, of being kissed mindless and feeling his naked body against hers?

No. She wanted to make the dream they had shared a reality. She wanted to experience for real what she'd only felt in that dream.

She moved back to the window and once again looked outside, waiting for him to return and knowing that if he did, she intended to get what she wanted from him.

As JARED JOGGED BACK to the room with their dinner in one paper sack, drinks in another and new clothes he'd bought at the discount store in a third, he marveled at the strength that flowed through his body. He felt better now than he had before the accident that had put him in the coma.

He glanced down at his arm where the strip of skin had been taken off. Throughout the day it had healed completely, leaving no trace of the wound that had been there.

It was amazing. Whatever Kenneth had injected into him had definitely been a superhealing agent. In the medical world it would be nothing short of a miracle, but in the hands of Kenneth and his cohorts it would be a disaster.

Soldiers on the battlefield could be given the injections and made into superwarriors and there was no doubt in his mind that Kenneth would sell the services to the highest bidder.

Just another issue to worry about, he thought as he slowed his pace. It worried him that he hadn't been able to contact his brother. He found it equally troublesome that he was hearing the thoughts of a man he didn't know and wasn't trying to tap in to.

He wasn't sure how long he and Willa would be safe at the motel and he still hadn't come up with another plan. *Willa.* Thoughts of her filled his head.

The day had not only been torturous because of his inability to contact Jack, but also because of Willa's presence in the small confines of the room.

Concentration had been difficult with her so close to him. He'd been acutely conscious of her tiniest sigh, of each and every movement she made. The scent of her had eddied in the air, stirring him in a way he'd never felt before.

He quickened his pace as he approached the motel.

She jumped up from the chair at the small table as he walked into the room. "What took you so long? I was worried."

"I took a small detour to the store." He threw the bag of clothing on the bed and then set the sacks with their meal on the table. "I got us each a change of clothes. I hope I was as good at guessing your sizes as you were at guessing mine."

She walked over to the bed and grabbed the plastic bag while he began to pull the burgers and fries and drinks from the sacks.

"They're clean, that's all I care about," she replied. She pulled out the pair of black sweatpants and the T-shirt he'd bought and smiled as she checked the sizes. "You got it right." She pulled out the pair of black lace panties with tiny red bows at the sides that he'd thrown in on impulse and he felt a sudden flush sweeping over him.

"I thought they matched the jogging pants," he said awkwardly. The truth was he'd spotted the black panties and instantly envisioned her in them.

"They're fine," she replied and then joined him at the table.

"I also got myself a clean T-shirt and jeans and both of us baseball hats," he said.

For a few minutes they ate in silence. Breakfast had been a long time ago and they were both hungry. As he watched her eat, tension coiled tight in his stomach. When she licked salt from her lips, he thought of how her lips had felt beneath his, so soft and so hot.

He didn't want to go there. It wouldn't be fair to her. Although he'd love to take away from all this a memory of tasting her skin, of making love to her, he loved her too much to do that to her.

He loved her. As crazy as it sounded, as new as the emotion was burning inside his chest, he recognized it as love. He'd had six months of being inside her head, of hearing her innermost thoughts and sharing her dreams and in that time he'd fallen in love with her.

Making love had been something he'd thought about, dreamed about in his years of captivity and if he only got to experience it once in his life, he would have chosen to have that experience with Willa.

But she'd had only a couple of days with him, days spent in danger and trauma. Besides, he was nothing more than an experiment and she deserved so much more than that.

"Tell me about your mother," he said suddenly, wanting, *needing* conversation that would take him away from his sensual thoughts.

She looked at him in surprise. "Why would you want to know about her?"

"Because you cared about her a lot, because you think about her often."

She took a sip of her soda and then leaned back in the chair, her expression soft and slightly pained. "Since it was always just the two of us we were very close. She liked to laugh and she had a wonderful sense of humor. She loved picnics and throwing parties and me. She was a terrific mom. When I was taking care of her through her illness I realized that was what I wanted to do for a living."

"You're very good at it," he said.

"I love what I do."

"You never tried to find your father?"

She shook her head. "I figured if he wanted to have a relationship with me he would have stuck around or at least stayed in contact. I always understood that he didn't want to be my mother's husband, but I never really understood why he didn't want to be my father."

"You'll make a wonderful mother someday," he observed.

She smiled then, one of her full open smiles that half stole his breath away. "I wanted that. I wanted at least two children. And while we're talking about wish lists, I also always wanted a dog. A big fluffy dog that would give lots of kisses and be a part of the family."

He realized she was talking in the past tense, as if she'd already abandoned those dreams, had already written a tragic ending for herself.

"Willa, you'll still have those things." He reached across the table and captured one of her hands with his. "You're going to get out of this mess and you'll find a man who loves you to distraction, a man who will give you the children you want and buy that big furry, loving dog for you."

She entwined her fingers with his and her eyes were more green than gray as she gazed at him. "What about you, Jared, what kind of dreams did you have?"

"My dreams aren't so different than yours," he replied. "I wanted time with my brother, time to see his face and touch his hand. I wanted a family and something normal and sane. I wanted barbecues in the backyard and quiet nights staring up at the stars."

"But right now there's just you and me." She caught her lower lip with her teeth and squeezed his fingers. "And all I can think about is how much I want you to make love to me."

He felt as if he stopped breathing for a long moment. He released her hand and got up from the table, as want battled with rationality.

"That's not a very good idea," he said. "It's just this crazy situation we find ourselves in that has you thinking about that."

"That's not true," she protested and got to her feet. "Jared, I want you and I know that you want me, too. You can pretend that you don't, but I know the truth."

Jared took a step back from her and fought for control. "Willa, don't you get it? I'm nothing but somebody's scientific experiment."

She looked appalled at his words. "Oh, Jared, you're so much more than that," she replied as she moved closer to him, so close the tips of her breasts touched his chest. His breath caught there as she reached up a hand and placed her palm on his cheek.

"You're the kindest, most gentle man I've ever known. You're smart and sexy and since the moment you were brought into the hospital broken and bleeding, I had a special connection to you."

"It's possible tonight or tomorrow Jack will show up and you'll never see me again," he said, barely maintaining his control by a thread. It was important that she understood the reality of the situation.

"And it's equally possible that by tonight or tomorrow Kenneth will find us and I'll be dead. You're my last meal, Jared, my final wish if I should die." She wrapped her arms around his neck and pressed herself against him, her eyes vivid green and luminous as she gazed up at him.

Desire, rich and thick, coursed through his veins and he was instantly fully aroused. Still, he struggled against giving in to that desire. *Just a kiss,* he thought. Maybe if he kissed her it would be enough.

He took her mouth with his and at the same time wrapped his arms around her. It was like holding fire in his arms—she burned him with her warmth, dizzied him with the smoke of her kiss.

Their tongues battled in a sensual war that only made his desire more intense. He tried to remember each and every new sensation he felt at the moment, the clean scent of her, the moist softness of her mouth and the press of her full breasts against him.

He'd only dreamed of this—of her and the reality of having her heart beating against his own, and the knowledge that if he wanted he could make the dream they had shared a reality was nearly overwhelming.

He broke the kiss with the intention of stepping back from her, of halting things before they careened out of control, but at that moment she slid her hands up the back of his shirt and moved her hips against his in a way that shattered the last of his control.

He groaned her name and had no idea if he said it out loud or mentally cried out to her. She responded in kind, his name a rumble of throaty passion that flamed inside him.

As they tumbled to the bed, he had a last thought that they were about to make a mistake, but it was a thought that couldn't be sustained as his mouth found hers once again.

Chapter Seven

With Jared's arms around her Willa easily forgot the fear that had been a part of her since the night she'd taken him from the hospital. Her desire for him filled her to the point where there was simply no room for any other emotion, good or bad. There was just him, filling her up.

His mouth took hers with a ravenous hunger and she responded with the same eagerness, loving the taste of him, the wildness that his lips contained.

Her hands slipped up the back of his T-shirt and across his taut back. His skin was warm and supple over the lean muscles that stretched and played beneath her fingertips.

Jared. His name sang in her heart.

Sweet Willa. You take my breath away.

His thought filled her head and only made the kisses and caresses more intimate. He was not only touching her body, but he was also touching her mind.

His mouth left hers and trailed down the length of her neck, kissing and nipping her skin with erotic intent. Each touch of his mouth shot electric currents through her.

If she'd worried at all that maybe he didn't want her, the black panties had put those concerns to rest. They had been a gift from a lover, not those of a man buying necessities. When she'd seen those panties she'd known how much he wanted her and that had given her the courage to reach out for what she wanted.

As their legs entwined, she found the brush of the denim irritating. She wanted to feel the heat of his bare flesh against hers.

They continued to kiss and she realized he wasn't going to take the lead, that she'd have to be the aggressor. It was an unusual part for her to play. She'd never been aggressive when it came to making love with Paul, but then again she'd never felt these kinds of intense, overwhelming feelings for Paul.

When her hands moved to the zipper of her jeans he froze and looked at her, his eyes blazing. "I want to be naked with you," she said, her voice with the huskiness of her desire.

"Yes, I want that, too." His voice was as equally husky as hers.

As she pulled off her jeans, he did the same, his breathing fast and labored. With her jeans kicked to the foot of the bed she pulled her T-shirt over her head. He yanked his off, as well, and they came back together clad only in their underwear.

His skin was hot and she felt her nipples hardening with the need to be touched by him. His rock-solid arousal pressed against her and she wanted him hard and fast and furious inside her. She slid a hand down to grip him, but he inched away from her.

Slow, Willa. I want to take it slow and easy. I want to savor you.

His thought in her head was the most erotic thing she'd ever felt and the idea that he wanted to savor her rocked a new wave of passion through her.

He gathered her into his arms and reached behind her to unfasten her bra. He pulled it from her and then gazed at her nakedness.

You are so beautiful. You absolutely take my breath away.

He seemed to have no idea how beautiful he was, with his chiseled chest and muscular shoulders. In just the span of two days his body had seemed to reshape itself with a new fitness that was hot and appealing.

He raised a hand and cupped one of her breasts and she gasped with pleasure as his thumb grazed the tip of her turgid nipple. He followed the path of his thumb with his mouth and a sweet rush of sensations made her entire body tremble.

He used his tongue on one nipple and then the other, sucking and licking as she thrashed her head back and forth in excitement.

Within minutes they had taken off their underwear and their caresses grew more intimate.

For what seemed like forever he savored her, tasting each and every inch of her skin, sliding his hands across her bare flesh and worshipping her inside her head with his thoughts.

She was ready for him, mindless with pleasure, when he finally poised himself between her thighs. She grabbed his buttocks to pull him closer and he moaned as he eased into her.

He froze and placed his hands on either side of her face, his expression one of exquisite joy. Tears blurred her vision as he began to rock his hips back and forth against hers.

Slowly at first, he stroked and moved against her and she writhed beneath him, lost in the act, in the man. Every muscle, each and every nerve ending, was on fire as she felt her peak rushing up to claim her.

Then it was on her, shuddering through her with a force that made her feel as if she were shattering. He cried out her name as she felt him stiffen against her and then he collapsed on the mattress next to her.

As she tried to catch her breath she heard none

of his thoughts in her head. She finally turned to look at him and found him gazing at her, a smile curving his gorgeous lips.

"Amazing," he finally breathed softly.

She returned his smile. "Yes, it was," she agreed.

He pulled her against him and kissed her forehead, the tip of her nose and finally her lips. They were the most tender kisses she'd ever received and her heart swelled full in her chest.

She cuddled against him, her brain wonderfully empty except for the scent of him and the warmth of his arms around her.

At the moment danger seemed very far away and she wanted nothing more than to remain snuggled in his arms. She didn't want to think about what had happened or speculate on what might happen next. She just wanted to be here with him.

He seemed to feel the same way for he made no move to get up from the bed, nor did he attempt to speak either aloud or inside her brain.

She lay with her head on his broad chest and he softly stroked her hair as their heartbeats finally found a slow, languid pace.

They hadn't used birth control. The sudden thought thundered in her head. It hadn't even entered her mind to use any kind of protection.

She'd stopped taking birth-control pills when she'd moved to Grand Forks from Kansas City.

There had been nobody in her life and she'd had no reason to think about it.

She thought about it now as she smoothed a hand across his chest. Could he even have children? With all the experiments that had been done with him perhaps he was sterile.

If the consequence to this night was an unexpected pregnancy she was surprised to realize she wouldn't mind. It hadn't been in her plans to be a single parent, but she knew without a doubt that if that was what happened she'd rise to the occasion and love the baby more than anyone on the face of the earth. If she were pregnant and if they managed to survive, she reminded herself.

"What are you thinking?" he asked, his chest rumbling beneath her ear.

She raised her head to look at him. "I thought you could tell."

He smiled. "I told you I'd try to stay out of your head unless you invited me in."

"I distinctly remember you being in my head a little while ago and I don't remember issuing an official invitation," she said teasingly.

He tightened an arm around her and his eyes gleamed bright. "Trust me, there was an invitation there somewhere."

She laid her head back down on his chest and released a deep, contented sigh. "It must be noisy in your head. How can you deal with all the racket of so many people's thoughts?"

"It's kind of like a radio. I can turn it up or down or even off if I want. It's the only way I could survive, otherwise I think I'd go insane."

"You're the most sane man I know," she said seriously. "And you must be incredibly strong, mentally, to have survived everything you've been through."

He smiled, but his gaze grew distant and she could only wonder what horrors he might be remembering. She slid from his arms and sat up.

"I'm going to go take a shower and put on my new panties," she said.

His smile grew just a little bit wicked. "I don't suppose you'd model them for me?"

"You might be able to talk me into a brief fashion show," she replied as she got off the bed and disappeared into the bathroom.

She felt languid, sated in a way she'd never had before. Making love with Jared was something she could definitely get used to if given the chance.

They had moved together as if they'd been lovers before, as if they knew each other's deepest desires, and the real thing had been far better than the dream they had shared.

She'd only been beneath the hot spray of water for a few minutes when she heard the shower curtain move aside and Jared stepped in. "I couldn't wait for the fashion show," he said as he plucked the bar of soap from her hand.

"Again?" she whispered as he pulled her into his arms and she felt his hardness against her.

"And again and again," he replied.

It was only later as Jared slept next to her that she realized she was falling in love with him. Her feelings were based on far more than just the sex they'd shared.

She loved his gentle nature and the sense of humor that sparkled in his eyes. He awed her with his inner strength and his absolute resolve to keep her safe even at his own expense. He was the man she'd been searching for, the man she'd like to share her life.

Yes, she was falling in love with him, but no matter how she twisted the situation they were in, inside her head she couldn't find a happy ending.

JACK MADDOX REACHED for his wife Claudia's hand as the others took their seats at the large dining-room table. They were in a hotel room just outside the Grand Forks city limits. They'd arrived that evening, flying in from Rapid City, South Dakota, to rendezvous with Drew Kincaid and his wife, Melinda, and Zack O'Hara with his fiancée, Kendra Sinclair. Two other members of the team, Matt Whitlock and Shelley Young, had been unable to make the trip because their son, Trevor, was sick with the flu.

The six of them had come to Grand Forks with one mission in mind—to find Jared. Jack had rented a three-bedroom suite in the upscale hotel to accommodate everyone. They were now all seated around the large dining-room table.

"This is what I know," he began as he released Claudia's hand. "Saturday Jared contacted me via the Web site." He nodded to Kendra, who had been responsible for utilizing the implanted knowledge of an eight-point star in order to contact other test subjects through the Web site she'd set up.

"He left a phone number for me to call and the phone belongs to a Willa Tyler, a nurse at Grand Forks Memorial Hospital," Jack continued. "For the past six months she's been particularly involved in a patient who has been in a coma."

"And you think that was Jared," Drew said.

Jack nodded. "It would explain why I couldn't contact him after we left The Facility."

Zack leaned forward, his intelligent brown eyes filled with concern. "So you think he came out of the coma and convinced this nurse to take him to her home?"

"That's what had to have happened. The only thing that would make Jared leave the hospital was if he thought he was in imminent danger," Jack said.

"Sykes," Kendra said, the name like a curse on her lips.

Kendra's father, Benjamin Stewart, had been Sykes's business partner years ago, until Sykes had crossed ethical lines and Benjamin had threatened to go to the authorities, then Sykes had killed him.

"Maybe Jared knew that Sykes was closing in, so he convinced this nurse to get him out of the hospital," she said.

"It's the only thing that makes sense," Claudia added.

"And so Jared contacted you and you called him on Willa's phone. What happened next?" Zack asked.

As an FBI agent who had been partly responsible for getting The Facility shut down, Jack knew that Zack would want all the facts on the table.

"He gave me Willa's address and it took me a while to arrange for somebody to pick him up. We didn't have anyone working here in town, but David Bahr was the closest in physical distance and agreed to come and get him." David Bahr was another test subject who had contacted them through the eight-point star Web site. He had been working with them to find Kenneth Sykes and ensure that he was put out of business forever.

Jack paused to take a sip of coffee and then continued. "When David reached Willa's house nobody was there."

"Any sign of a break-in or trouble?" Drew asked.

"No, nothing." Jack felt an overwhelming frustration threatening to take hold of him. *Jared, where are you? What happened to you after we spoke on the phone? We were so close—so close to being united again.*

"And there's been nothing from Willa or Jared since Saturday?" Zack tapped the side of his head. "You haven't been able to pick up anything from him?"

"No. I'm hoping what happened is that maybe Jared sensed danger approaching and he and Willa took off. He told me Sykes was in town, so maybe he decided that he and Willa had to move before David could get there." He refused to consider the possibility that Sykes had somehow managed to find them at the Tyler house.

"Maybe they're both dead," Drew said, speaking Jack's deepest fear aloud.

"I don't think so," Jack replied. "I think if they were dead their bodies would have been found. Sykes would have wanted me to know that he'd won where Jared was concerned. He would have left their bodies where they were sure to be found."

His hand tightened around his coffee cup as he thought of the man who had held them captive for so many years, a man who would leave Jared's body in plain sight just to let Jack know that ultimately Jared hadn't been able to escape.

"Have you tried calling Willa's phone number again?" Zack asked.

"Yeah, several times, but there's no answer. It rings a couple of times and then goes to her voice mail and I don't want to leave a message in case she's no longer in possession of the phone."

"So where do we go from here?" Drew asked.

"I know where I'm going," Melinda replied. "I'm sorry, but I really need to go to bed."

"Are you okay?" Drew asked.

"I'm fine," she assured him with a smile. "I'm just exhausted. Don't worry, everything is all right." She touched her stomach and then got up from the table and went into the bedroom where she and Drew would be staying for the duration of their time in Grand Forks.

"That's normal, right?" Drew asked when Melinda had closed the bedroom door.

Kendra gave him a reassuring smile. "It's almost eleven at night and she's pregnant. Tired is very normal."

"So he hasn't tried to access the Web site again?" Zack asked.

"No, there's been no further activity there," Jack said with a look at Kendra for confirmation. She nodded.

"What's our plan?" Zack got up from the table, as if unable to sit still another minute.

Jack frowned thoughtfully. He only wished he had a surefire plan to find his brother. "There isn't much that can be done tonight, but starting first thing in the morning I want us all to begin searching for them. We'll check all the motels, check in at the hospital and see if we can get a list of Willa's friends. I'm hoping they are still here, that Jared knows we'll be looking around the area where he disappeared."

"So the best thing we can all do is get a good night's sleep," Drew said as he got up from his chair.

"I appreciate you all coming here to help," Jack said.

"You know we'll do whatever it takes to save Jared," Drew exclaimed.

"And take down Sykes," Zack added, his features dark with suppressed emotion.

It took only minutes for everyone except Claudia and Jack to leave the dining area and disappear into their bedrooms.

Jack got up from the table and walked to the window that looked down on the parking lot below. After six months of searching, he'd come so close to being reunited with his twin brother. When he'd heard Jared's voice on the phone he'd felt as if a piece of himself had been restored. But now Jared seemed further away than he'd ever been.

"We'll find them," Claudia said softly as she

came to stand just behind him. She placed a comforting hand on his back.

He turned to look at her, loving the silk of her dark blond hair and the chocolate-brown of her eyes. She'd been his salvation. Their love had been the balm that had soothed the darkness that had been Jack's life.

In the years that he had spent as Kenneth's special project, captive in The Facility, he'd only dreamed of a woman like her.

Fate had dropped him not only into her life, but also into her bed when he'd escaped from The Facility. Unfortunately he'd been suffering a drug-induced amnesia and it had taken him opening his heart to Claudia for the memories of his twin brother to surface.

"I'm going to bed," she said. "Are you coming?"

"In a few minutes," he replied. He leaned down and kissed her, as always amazed by the luck that had brought her into his life.

They murmured their good-nights and then Claudia went into their adjoining bedroom and Jack turned back to face the window.

Kenneth's injections and experiments had transformed each of the men who had been in the room earlier. Drew possessed a superhealing ability and Kendra and Zack had discovered that when together they had the power of telekinesis. Jared had been the only person Jack was able to mentally communicate with as Jack's real ability was precognition.

Unfortunately his ability to see his future with his brother wasn't working. No vision came to him promising a happy ending, nor did he have any visions of impending doom. It was as if the ending hadn't been written yet and therefore couldn't be seen.

As he thought of Kenneth Sykes, the man whom they had called Uncle Ken, the man who was responsible for so much grief and despair, he balled his hands into fists.

He could kill him, but he wouldn't. They needed Kenneth alive to find out his plans for taking his research elsewhere. Jack and his team, including the FBI, were committed to stopping Kenneth before he did any further damage.

He leaned his forehead against the cool glass. He'd meant it when he told the others that he didn't think his brother and Willa Tyler were dead. He simply refused to believe that Jared was no longer on this earth, that a happy reunion was no longer possible.

Zack had worked undercover at The Facility and his contact had been Kendra, who had been working there under the name of Kendra Sinclair and feeding the FBI information. When they managed to escape, Zack and his buddies in the FBI had finally managed to locate The Facility, which had been housed in old government barracks hidden deep in the limestone caves of South Dakota.

When the FBI had burst in, Jack had desperately hoped they'd find Jared there, that Kenneth had recaptured him before he could get away. But instead they had found that the place had been cleaned out. The research and all of the experimentees were gone, as if none of it had ever existed in the first place.

The most chilling thing that had been found was the discovery of a dead woman in one of the freezers. It appeared that she had been pregnant at the time of her death and the unborn baby had been removed.

The fear that Kenneth was taking his research and testing to the next level was profound. He was attempting to create a new generation to experiment on and the thought chilled Jack to the bone.

In the six months since the brothers had made their escape on that cold November night, Jack had blessed his luck in finding Claudia and being able to begin to build a real life for himself. But in those six months, every moment of happiness he'd had had been tempered by Jared's absence.

Jared, where are you? He opened his mind in an attempt to hear any contact his brother might be attempting, but there was nothing and it was that absolute silence in his head that he found so terrifying.

Chapter Eight

There was a moment when Willa left sleep behind and yet wasn't fully awake, a moment when the only thought in her mind was the warmth of Jared's arms around her and the steady sweet beat of his heart against her own.

She felt safe and loved in his arms and the loneliness that had plagued her life for the past year was banished. Making love to him had been amazing. He'd been a generous, thoughtful lover and had stirred a depth of emotion in her she'd never felt before.

If only they could stay this way forever, wrapped in bedsheets that held their scent and cuddled together in a sleepy embrace.

All too quickly that moment passed and the reality of their situation slammed into her with a startling blow. They either had to check out of the motel this morning or pay for another day.

So far this small room had felt like a safe haven, but would they be pushing their luck by remaining here for another night? And if so, where did they go from here?

A glance at the clock told her it was just after five in the morning. Knowing she wouldn't go back to sleep, she slid from his arms, glad that he didn't stir from his slumber.

She padded into the tiny bathroom and closed the door, then stood for a long moment in front of the mirror and stared at her reflection.

It was hard to believe how normal her life had been a mere four days before, that the biggest thing she feared was that she'd always be lonely and the man in the coma might never wake up. Now she had to worry about mad scientists and bald men with guns.

There had been a second when they'd been making love that she'd felt Jared's love for her. It had not only been in the intimacy of his touch, but also in his thoughts that invaded her head.

He loved her and if she were to search the very depths of her heart she would acknowledge that she loved him, too. She knew it was crazy, that they'd only really known each other for less than four days, and yet the connection felt as if it had been forged over months, even years.

She filled the sink with tepid water and then scooped it up to wash her face, trying to gain some perspective. Loving Jared should be an uncomplicated thing, but it felt extremely complicated.

One way or another he was going to pass through her life. He had bigger issues to deal with than love. In a sense he was on a mission to save the world and she was simply a nurse who had momentarily rocketed into his path.

There was no real place for her in his future—if he had a future, and she'd be a fool to think otherwise. She started the water in the shower and stepped beneath the hot spray.

As she lathered and rinsed, her mind worked over all that had happened since the moment she'd walked into the hospital room and discovered he was not only conscious, but also frantic to get out of the hospital.

How she wished she could just pick up the phone and call her mother, hear the sound of her voice and listen to whatever wisdom she had to give. But, of course, there was nobody they could call to get them out of this mess.

Her heart skipped a beat as her brain suddenly whirled with a possibility. Had they overlooked a key item that might be the most efficient way to contact Jack?

Quickly she shut off the water, grabbed a towel and wrapped it around herself and then hurried out of the bathroom, her heart thundering with the possibility.

She turned on the lamp and sat on the edge of the bed. "Jared?"

He shot up to a sitting position, his eyes bleary with sleep. "What? What's going on?" He tensed, as if expecting danger.

"Relax, as far as I know everything is okay, but I just had a thought."

The tenseness of his muscles eased and he glanced at the clock and then back at her. "A thought at five o'clock in the morning?"

She nodded. "I woke up and couldn't get back to sleep. I was in the shower wishing that I could call my mother and then I realized something. My cell phone."

He frowned and rubbed a hand over his short hair. "What about it?"

"Jack called you on it. Maybe he's been trying to reach you that way again." She reached for his sleep-warmed hand and grabbed it. "We have to go back to my house and get it. It must have fallen out of my pocket when we were trying to make our way out of the gas. It's probably lying on the living-room floor right now."

He sat up straighter, his gaze locked with hers. "It's possible Kenneth or one of his men picked it up."

"But it's also possible they didn't. We have to go back there, Jared. Since you haven't been able to connect with him using your mind, maybe he can connect with you in the more conventional way."

"It would be dangerous for us to go back there," he said thoughtfully.

A small burst of laughter released itself from her. "I'd say right now anything we might do is dangerous. At least if we can get that phone we might be closer to uniting you with Jack." For the first time in two days a ray of hope shone in Willa's heart.

"I could go by myself and leave you here," he said more to himself than to her. He pulled his hand from hers. "You would be safe here for the length of time it took me to get in and then get out of your house."

"No way," she replied firmly. "We're partners in this, Jared. Where you go, I go. Besides, I know the inside of my house better than you do. It makes sense for me to go in and for you to be my watchdog outside."

"I don't like it," he said flatly.

She smiled. "To be honest, I'd rather have a couple of my teeth extracted, but it has to be done. It might be our best chance of contacting Jack."

"I can think of lots of things I'd rather do," he said and his gaze slid slowly, heatedly, down the towel she wore.

Warmth torched through her but she steadfastly ignored it. "Get that thought right out of your head. We have work to do and right now that's the most important thing on our agenda."

He sighed. "You're right." He moved his long

legs over the side of the bed and rose like a beautiful, naked Adonis. "I'll shower and then we'll figure out how this is going to work."

As Jared took his shower Willa dressed in the new jogging pants and black T-shirt that he'd bought for her the evening before. The panties felt like a sinful indulgence, but she figured if she was going to die today she'd like to be wearing a sexy pair of panties bought by a man who wanted her.

By the time she finished dressing and had finger-combed her hair as best she could, he was out of the bathroom and getting dressed in his new, clean clothes.

"The first thing we need to do is to decide if we want to stay here another night," she said once he was dressed and they were seated at the table.

She couldn't help but notice how hot he looked in the black T-shirt that pulled across his shoulders. His biceps seemed to grow bigger each time she looked at them. His jeans hugged his long legs and slim hips like a second skin.

"At the moment I don't sense any danger in remaining here," he said. "And I'm not sure where we'd go if we did leave," he added, echoing her earlier thoughts.

"So we stay," she said. "I'll go to the office and pay for another night and then we can head over to my house."

"How far away are we from your house?" he asked. "I don't know the city of Grand Forks at all."

"About a fifteen-minute cab ride," she replied. "Pretty much everything in the city is just a fifteen- or twenty-minute cab ride away."

"Then you go pay for another night and I'll call for a cab to pick us up." He gave her the rest of the money.

She picked it up, shoved it into her back pocket and then stood. "I'll be right back."

The spring morning air was chilly and she hurried toward the office, unsure if it was the air that made her feel unusually cold or the thought of what could happen when they tried to get back into her house.

What if somebody was waiting there for them? What if she and Jared walked into an ambush? Her heart beat a rapid tattoo as she entered the office. Within minutes she had paid the night clerk, who was still on duty, for another night and was on her way back to their room.

When she walked in Jared greeted her at the door. "The cab should be here within the next ten minutes or so," he said.

"We'll have the driver drop us off on the street behind my house," she said. "Then I can go in through the back and hopefully nobody will know I'm there. You can wait outside and if you hear anyone coming you can let me know." She tapped her head. "I'm definitely giving you permission to get inside my head for this."

He stepped closer to her and placed his palms on either side of her face as his amazing blue eyes held hers in an intense gaze. *I don't know what I'd do if anything happened to you.*

She covered his hands with hers. *You have to promise me that if anything happens to me, if we get split up for any reason, you'll continue to try to connect with your brother and you'll find a way to stop Sykes before he can hurt anyone else.*

She could tell by the look in his eyes that he didn't want to make the promise, but it was important to her that he did.

Dropping her hands to her side, she stepped back from him. "Jared, if you don't do that then all of this has been for nothing. You have to stop him, no matter what happens to me, no matter what happens to us. You can't let him get out of the States, where nobody might ever find him and he can continue hurting people. Promise me, Jared."

He nodded. "Okay, I promise." He pulled her back into his arms. "You know I'm in love with you, Willa."

Before she could respond, a horn honked out front. The cab had arrived.

THE CAB LET THEM OUT on the street behind Willa's house. The morning sun had risen and people would be enjoying breakfast together before sending the kids off to school and heading to their jobs for the day.

Jared wondered what it would be like to have that kind of life, to have that kind of normalcy with a woman like Willa. Hell, what was he thinking? He didn't want a woman *like* Willa—he wanted her.

As they walked through the yard of the house directly behind Willa's place he shoved those kinds of thoughts out of his mind and instead opened it up to receive the thoughts of others in the area.

A cacophony of noise immediately filled his brain. Over the years he had grown adept at picking and sorting through the chaos to find what he sought. At the moment he heard nothing that caused him alarm.

They stopped on the back edge of her property and crouched down behind a large, flowering bush. "How are you going to get inside?" he asked, knowing she didn't have her house keys.

"There's a ceramic frog in that little flower bed next to the patio and there's a back-door key inside his belly," she said. She smiled at him, a smile of forced bravado. She looked gorgeous even with her silky blond hair tucked up inside the ball cap he'd bought. "Are you picking up anything?"

"Your neighbor to the left is having an affair

with a woman named Angela and somebody in the house on the other side is wondering why their dog has been throwing up for the past two days."

"Wait. Jim is having an affair?" She looked astonished.

Jared smiled, hoping the gesture masked his concern. "If you're going to go, go now."

She didn't waste time, but took off running toward the back of the house. As she reached the flower bed and picked up the frog, Jared kept his gaze shooting first in one direction, then another, looking for anyone who might do her harm.

He kept his mind open, other people's thoughts rushing through at a speed that was almost impossible to process. At the back door she turned and gave him a thumbs-up, then used the key and disappeared inside.

Jared's heart pounded in his chest with fear for her. Surely if somebody had been inside the house then he would have picked up something. But he didn't trust his ability as much as he had before the coma.

It worried him that he couldn't make contact with Jack. He wondered if there had been some sort of brain damage while he'd been in the coma. And yet the fact that he could read the minds of everyone in the neighborhood belied the fact of any damage.

Maybe Jack was still too far away, he told himself. He hadn't asked Jack where he was located in the brief phone conversation they'd shared. For all he knew Jack could be a thousand miles away and Jared's ability to read his brother's mind, to head-talk with his brother, was only good if they were within close range of each other.

Jared, they fixed my front window. Willa's thought filled his head. *It's amazing. All the glass has been cleaned up and there's no evidence that anything happened in here.*

Just find your phone and get out of there, he replied. He wasn't surprised that they'd fixed the window. They wouldn't want to draw any undue attention to the house, to what had taken place inside.

As the minutes ticked by, Jared's anxiety increased. Adrenaline coursed through him as he waited. What was taking so long?

She's here! I can grab her and prove myself to Kenneth!

The thought exploded in Jared's head at the same time he saw the man slide around the corner of the house and head for the unlocked back door.

Willa! Get out now! Run out the front door and head to the motel. I'll meet you there. He frantically telegraphed those thoughts as he recognized the man. He was the little worm in the white lab coat who had brought the instruments into the room for Kenneth at the old abandoned psychiatric hospital. George, that was what Kenneth had called him.

Jared had no idea if Willa had gotten his frantic thoughts or if she had instantly obeyed the command. He barreled forward toward the man as he made it to the open back door.

The man never heard Jared coming. He gasped in surprise as Jared grabbed him by his shirt and yanked him backward. The two men tumbled to the brick patio, where the man pulled a wicked knife from his pocket.

Jared grabbed his wrist and slammed his hand against the bricks, and the knife released and skittered across to the flower bed on the other side.

George was small but he was wiry and it took all of Jared's strength to finally manage to straddle him.

"Please," he gasped as Jared's hands circled his scrawny neck. "Please don't kill me. I wasn't going to hurt her, I was just going to ask her where you were."

"Looks like you've found me," Jared replied, fighting the desire to squeeze the life out of the man. "Where's Kenneth?" he asked.

"I don't know. I swear I don't know. When we left that old hospital we all went our separate ways." A sob escaped him. "All I've got is a phone number. Just don't kill me, okay?"

"Who knows you're here?" Jared tightened his grip on the man's throat. "Who did you tell that Willa was here?"

"Nobody! I didn't get a chance to tell anyone." He choked and coughed.

Jared looked deep into his mind, read the thoughts that were flying like frantic butterflies. A man who believed he was about to die had all kinds of things running through his head.

I knew this was all going to end badly. I'm not ready to die. Who's going to take care of my cat? I should have told somebody I was coming here.

It was the last thought that made Jared realize he was telling the truth. He hadn't yet told anyone that Willa was back at her house.

"I want you to give Kenneth a message for me," Jared said. "You tell him that I'm leaving town, that Willa doesn't know where I'm going, that nobody knows. We came here to get some money, and then I'm out of her life. She doesn't know anything about what's happened except for what Kenneth told her. You got that?"

Tears oozed from the man's eyes as he tried to nod his head. "Yes, yes, I've got it," he gasped.

Jared released his throat with one hand and reared back and slammed his fist into the man's chin, rendering him unconscious.

That would buy Jared enough time to get inside

and make sure Willa had escaped the house. He raced through the back door and called her name.

No reply. The front door stood open and he breathed a sigh of relief. She must have heard him telling her to get out and had run.

Unless somehow the unconscious creep on the back patio had lied with his thoughts. Unless somehow he was another of Kenneth's experiments who had the capacity to fool Jared.

The thought terrified him. Had somebody been inside waiting for Willa or him to return? While he'd been grappling with the creep on the patio, had somebody grabbed Willa and taken her away?

Oh, God, let him be wrong. His heart thundered in his chest as he checked each room in the house and found them empty. He then raced out the front door, inwardly screaming her name.

His legs pumped, carrying him down the sidewalk. He had no money for a cab and in any case this residential neighborhood wouldn't be where cabbies regularly parked to wait for a fare.

He didn't have a way back to the motel except the power of his own feet and the desperation that drove him. Thankfully he'd paid attention to the route the cab driver had taken from their motel.

Willa? Are you there?

When there was no reply he felt as if he might throw up. Dear God, he'd known this was a bad idea the moment she'd brought it up and yet he'd reluctantly agreed to it.

And now he didn't know if Willa was dead or alive. The pain that rocked through him was like none he'd ever felt before. It stole his breath and threatened to buckle his knees, but he pushed on, fear sizzling through him as he ran.

He'd told her he loved her and they hadn't even had a chance to talk about it. She hadn't even gotten an opportunity to respond.

She'd been the light that had pulled him from the darkness of his coma. Her very thoughts had been what had caused him to fight for life rather than give in to death. He loved her and the thought of her in trouble or dead nearly destroyed him. He'd done this to her. He should have never involved her in all this. He should have just let Kenneth find him in the hospital.

He finally reached a main street and stopped to catch his breath. His gaze shot first in one direction and then the other, seeking a cab he could grab. He'd worry about paying for the ride later. His sole concern was getting to the motel room to see if she was there.

He ran with a single-minded purpose, his mind emptied of all thoughts as his body worked overtime to take him where he needed to go.

Willa. His heart cried her name and a grief like

he'd never felt filled him. He loved her and now he feared that he'd never see her beautiful face again, would never hold her in his arms again.

He finally stopped at a corner, his breath nearly gone and a hitch in his side that made it impossible to go farther without taking a moment to rest.

As he drew in a deep breath he mentally called to her once again. *Willa,* his heart cried out.

Jared, I'm here. I'm safe and on my way to the motel to wait for you.

Her voice exploded in his head and the sweet sound of it cast him to his knees and he wept like a baby.

Chapter Nine

Willa stood at the window of the motel, her heart banging against her ribs as she waited for Jared's return. She'd been afraid, so very afraid that whoever had shown up at the house had managed to overwhelm him.

When she'd heard his warning, she'd shot out the front door and had run faster than she'd ever run in her life. Fear had screamed through her, blocking out all other thought other than the need to get away.

She'd run until she couldn't run anymore and then thankfully had managed to flag down a cab. It was only when she was safe inside the motel room that the fear had ebbed and she'd heard his frantic thoughts and had let him know she was safe.

More important, she knew he was safe and on his way back to the motel. She clutched her cell phone tightly in her hand. She'd found it on the floor just under the edge of the sofa right before Jared had told her to get out of the house.

He loved her. That was what he'd told her just before they had gotten into the cab to go to her house. She hadn't even had a chance to reply.

And how would she have replied? She leaned her head against the sun-warmed glass and considered the question. She loved him. She loved him more than she'd ever loved a man, more than she thought it possible that she would ever love anyone else. But that love came with a hefty price tag.

If she told Jared she loved him, then she would be agreeing to throw her life in with his, to share his future with him, but at the moment there was no way to guess that future.

He had no home, he had no friends and his only family was a man as equally at risk. Until Kenneth was caught and put in jail Jared and his brother were effectively fugitives from life.

Was that what she wanted in her future? Was she willing to give up her home, her job and what friends she'd made in the town of Grand Forks for an uncertain future with a man she'd really only known for three days?

As the cab pulled up in front of the room and Jared stepped out of the vehicle, her heart swelled at the sight of him. She went outside to pay the driver. Jared had mentally told her minutes before that he'd managed to grab a cab to bring him the rest of the way home.

They didn't speak until they were both back in the room, and then he didn't say a word but instead wrapped her up in an embrace that nearly stole her breath away.

He buried his face in the crook of her neck and drew a deep, shuddering breath. "I thought something had happened to you," he whispered. "I thought I'd lost you."

"I'm okay, we're okay," she replied, her chest aching as she realized the depth of the emotion inside him. "I got the cell phone."

"To hell with the cell phone." His voice was a raspy growl as he continued to hold her tight. "I don't know what I'd do if anything happened to you."

"You know what you'd do," she replied as she tightened her arms around his neck. "You'd go on, because you have to, because you promised me you would."

Finally he released his hold on her and she stepped back from him and held up the cell phone. "I've had ten missed calls that were from an unknown number."

"Is that unusual?" His eyes still radiated with raw emotion.

"Definitely. They have to be from Jack. I think he's been trying to get in touch with us again. The last call came in about forty-five minutes ago. Surely he'll try again soon. Jared, it might just be a few hours before you're with your brother."

He continued to hold her gaze. "And what about us?" His voice was soft and held an unspoken plea. He stepped closer to her. "When Jack gets here come with us." He reached out a hand to her. "I love you, Willa. I know I shouldn't want to bring you into my crazy life, but the idea of not having you with me hurts more than anything I've ever felt."

He pulled her back into his arms. "Tell me, Willa. Tell me that you love me, too." He seemed to be holding his breath as he waited for her reply.

Willa knew she had a choice and she searched the depths of her heart before giving him an answer. Was he simply an exciting panacea for the loneliness that had plagued her life since her mother's death?

No, as she stared up at him she knew that what she felt wasn't just a passing fancy, a break from the boredom. It was the kind of love that could make a woman give up her life for uncertainty, the kind to last a lifetime if allowed to flourish.

"I love you, too," she said softly and once again found herself caught against his chest in an embrace. She closed her eyes as he held her and wondered if they were both crazy.

"I knew it, I knew that you loved me," he said, his voice a fervent whisper.

Instead of feeling joyous, she felt like crying. What good did it do to love each other in the mess they were in? What kind of future could they plan together when they didn't even know where they'd be the next day?

"Willa?" He held her away from him and looked down at her. "We'll be okay. We're going to make it work," he said as if he understood all the concerns that flitted around in her head.

"We'll have that life you've always dreamed of, with the furry dog and the kids and friends who come over for barbecues. We'll have quiet nights watching television and once a week we'll have a date night."

He was telling her about the things she'd dreamed of while she'd sat next to him in the hospital. He was repeating her thoughts as she'd watched him breathe, prayed for him to wake up from the coma that held him so still.

"What we have is magical, Willa," he said, his eyes glowing an electric blue. "Trust me. Trust in us."

She was helpless to do anything else. Her love for him made her believe all things were possible, that they would somehow get through this and have the life she'd always dreamed of.

"All we need is a phone call," she said as she

stepped out of his arms and sat on the edge of the bed, the cell phone clutched tightly in her hand.

He sat next to her and put an arm around her shoulder. "Maybe he'll call soon."

"And then what?" she asked.

"He takes us someplace where we'll be safe and we figure things out from there."

She laid her head on his shoulder and hoped that it was as easy as that. But she had a terrible feeling that it wasn't going to be that easy, that it was quite possible the worst still lay ahead.

KENNETH STOOD AT the window of the downtown hotel, staring out into the late afternoon sun. He was normally a man well in control of his emotions, but at the moment anger of mammoth proportions threatened to explode inside him.

The fact that Jared and his pretty nurse had managed to escape from the psychiatric hospital had sparked a flame of rage inside him that had been simmering for six months, ever since Jared and Jack had gotten away from him and The Facility.

He now clenched his fists at his sides. The twins' escape had destroyed years of work. The Facility had been the perfect place to conduct his experiments. The old government barracks in the limestone caves of South Dakota had been isolated and forgotten by everyone. Tons of money had gone in to building the labs, the cells and the amenities that housed the employees and the experiment subjects.

Everything had been abandoned when the twins had escaped. Kenneth hadn't been able to take the chance that they wouldn't talk. It had been a good thing that he'd been cautious and had moved out of The Facility because it hadn't taken long for the FBI to move in.

Apparently Jack had managed to convince some powerful people to listen to his story. Since then the heat had been on Kenneth. Ungrateful bastards, both of them, Jared and his brother, Jack.

He should have left Grand Forks the minute he'd realized Jared and Willa had managed to escape from the hospital where he'd set up a makeshift operation, but two things had kept him in town.

The first was that he'd thought that it would be relatively easy to pick them up again considering Jared had no money and no place to go and Kenneth's men had covered not only Willa's house and bank accounts, but also the homes of her friends from the hospital.

He wanted Jared back in his control, wanted to see what the latest injection had done to him, and he was also hoping that the foreign investors would get it together in the next week or two and allow him to take his research overseas. Things had become too hot in the United States and in any case Kenneth had no allegiance to anyone, except whoever would pony up the most money and allow his work to continue.

Turning away from the window, he walked over to the phone and rang for room service. Although it was a bit early for dinner he decided to go ahead and order, knowing that it often took a long time to get a meal delivered.

Once he'd ordered he returned to the window, aware that the gnawing in the pit of his stomach was probably frustration rather than hunger.

Damn them all for screwing everything up when they should have been grateful to be a part of a science that was so magnificent.

It had been years ago that Kenneth had discovered the reality of the recessive gene that some people carried, a gene that could be manipulated to heighten abilities. He'd named the gene I for Ideal and had begun his work to create the ideal man. During his early research he'd also learned that the manipulation of the gene worked best in young subjects.

It had been a coup for him after some shady legal maneuvering to gain custody of the twin boys after their parents' deaths when they'd only been five years old.

They had been his biggest successes and ultimately his greatest failures. They should have felt honored to be part of such amazing, cutting-edge studies. They should have been honored to sacrifice the rest of their lives in the name of Kenneth's brilliant work.

Now they would be sacrificed in the name of salvaging the damage they had done—in the name of science they had to be eliminated.

He clenched his hands into fists, a fury building once again inside him. Where could they be hiding? Who might be helping Jared and Willa?

He had no idea where Jack might be despite the six months of hunting for him. Kenneth was a man who liked control and at the moment he felt his control spiraling away.

Jared and Jack hadn't been the only betrayal. Kendra Sinclair, one of the scientists working for him, had not only been his old partner's daughter, but had also been working with an undercover FBI agent who had infiltrated The Facility.

Then, of course, there were the experiments he'd considered failures. Some of them had been children he'd abducted and then let go, others had died or never recovered memories of the experiments that had been done to them.

Kenneth had come too far to let all his research be for naught. He would do whatever it took to protect himself and the work.

He'd already heard from George Lathrop, one of his lab assistants who, unbeknownst to Kenneth, had been staking out Willa's house. He'd told Kenneth that Jared had come to the house so that Willa could get some money and he could get out of town. Jared had assured the lab rat that Willa knew nothing about what was going on, that she'd just been a pawn he'd used to initially escape from the hospital.

Kenneth wasn't sure what he believed. It was quite possible Jared was telling the truth, that Willa knew nothing about the experiments or Jared's special abilities.

A knock on the door sounded and he turned from the window and walked over to peer out the security peephole. He couldn't be too careful. By now it was possible the FBI knew that he was in town.

He relaxed when he saw White, one of his newer soldiers, someone he'd worked with since Red had committed suicide several months before. White's greatest trait was his unrelenting loyalty to Kenneth and his desire to do anything and everything Kenneth instructed him to do, without question.

Kenneth unlocked the door and White entered. He was a big burly man with normal, pleasant features and a smile that rarely left his face.

"We found him," he said without preamble.

Excitement flooded through Kenneth. "Where?"

"The Moonlight Motel, about fifteen minutes

from here. One of our men spotted him leaving a fast-food restaurant and going into one of the motel's units."

"Was he alone?"

White nodded.

Kenneth walked over to the desk and picked up a large black leather bag. Inside were the items he would need to take more samples from Jared and the drug that would kill him and his pretty girl-friend if she was still with him.

"Let's go," he said and stepped out of the room. His blood sang in his veins. Within twenty minutes the loose end known as Jared would be no more.

Chapter Ten

Jared sat straight up in the bed, his heart thudding a rhythm of fear. He gazed around the room, seeking the source of his unease.

Afternoon sunshine seeped around the edges of the curtains at the window. Willa lay sleeping next to him, her nakedness stirring him even though they had made love only two hours earlier and had fallen asleep when they were finished.

He slid from the bed and reached for his pants on the floor. He stepped into them and went to the window and slid back the curtain so he could see the parking lot.

There was nothing to cause the flight-or-fight adrenaline that flooded his veins. The cars that were parked on either side of their unit were the same that had been there throughout the day.

He allowed the curtain to fall back into place and turned to look at Willa. Even in sleep she moved him, not just on a physical level, but in a deeply profound way.

For so many months, before he'd come out of the coma, she'd been with him, he'd been inside her dreams, privy to her thoughts. It had been then, before he'd seen her beauty, before he'd touched the silkiness of her hair, that he'd fallen in love with her soul.

He had no idea what his future held, but he couldn't imagine her not in it. When she'd told him she loved him he'd felt complete in a way he'd only dreamed about.

She owned his heart more than anyone ever had or ever would. He fought the impulse to stroke his hand across the softness of her hair, to kiss the lips that were now parted slightly in slumber.

He'd gone after an early dinner and then one thing had led to another and they had fallen into bed. There had been not only a hunger in their embrace, but also a kind of desperation that spoke of their uncertain future.

He wished he could offer her a future fit for a queen, with a palace to live in and every wish she'd ever had fulfilled. But the truth was he had nothing to offer her, nothing but his love. There was some comfort in knowing that for Willa, that seemed to be enough.

He picked up his T-shirt and pulled it over his

head and it was at that moment the random thought flew into his head.

This time he won't get away. I'll get the samples I need from him and then leave his body in the motel room to be found later.

Kenneth! Jared knew his nemesis was close— far too close—and if Jared didn't get Willa out of the room as soon as possible he would be on them.

"Willa!" He leaned over and shook her by the shoulder. She came awake instantly, as if responding in her sleep to the urgency in his voice.

"What's wrong?" she asked as her gaze shot to the floor where her clothes lay in a pile.

"They're coming. We have to go."

Her eyes flared with fear as she scrambled off the bed and hurriedly dressed. While she was doing that Jared gathered what little they had into one of the plastic shopping bags.

When he was finished and she was dressed he gestured her toward the bathroom. She looked at him questioningly. "We need to go out the window. They're really close now."

He was surprised that Kenneth wasn't blocking his thoughts from Jared. The fact that Kenneth wasn't blocking spoke of the man's out-of-control rage.

When they got into the bathroom he raised the window and knocked out the screen, then helped her up and over the ledge and to the ground outside.

Kenneth's thoughts grew stronger, making Jared fear that at any moment they would burst through the door of the motel.

He quickly crawled through the window and hit the ground, then grabbed her hand and together they took off running, attempting to put as much distance as possible between themselves and the motel.

They raced down one street and then another. He felt her terror radiating from her hand to his, heard it in the quick gasps she emitted as they ran for their lives.

He didn't allow them to stop and rest until he could no longer hear Kenneth's thoughts. It was only then he felt they were safe enough and far enough away to take a moment to get their bearings.

He pulled her behind a row of hedges in someone's yard and they both collapsed onto the ground. Although she said nothing he didn't have to be a mind reader to know what she was thinking.

Where did they go from here? What happened next? Why hadn't Jack called the cell phone? Her questions were his own, but he hated to admit to her that he didn't know what to do next.

He'd hoped that by this time Jack would have called and made arrangements to have them picked up. He'd hoped that before another night passed he and Willa would be safe with Jack.

"I know where we can go," she said suddenly.

He looked at her in surprise. "Where?"

"The hospital. There's an old storage room in a wing that isn't used much anymore. It connects to the rest of the hospital but has an outside door."

"A locked door?" he asked.

"Yes, but it opens with a keypad and I know the numeric code to punch in."

He frowned thoughtfully. "I don't know, Willa. It sounds risky to me. If you know the code then surely others do, as well."

"Only a handful and nobody uses that as an entrance. It's in the back and not convenient to the parking area. What other choice do we have, Jared? It's far too risky for us to stay out on the streets and checking in to another motel seems dangerous, as well."

As he stared into the depths of her blue eyes a crashing guilt descended upon him. What had he gotten her into? She deserved better than this, running for her life with a man who had no future plans, a man who had no past she could really understand. He'd walked out of the hospital and had waltzed her right into danger's arms. What kind of man did that to the woman he loved?

"Willa, I should have never gotten you into all this," he said.

She instantly leaned toward him and pressed a finger to his lips to still whatever else he might say.

"Shh, I don't want to hear any more. It's my choice to be here with you." She got to her feet. "Come on, let's head to the hospital."

He got up and in that moment he knew that he loved her enough that he would die for her. It was a strangely empowering feeling, to know that despite everything that had been done to him, despite the horrible past he'd had, he had the capacity to love that deeply, that strongly.

They began to walk again, keeping to side streets and on alert for Kenneth and his men. The cell phone weighed heavily in Jared's pocket and as he walked he sent out thoughts to his brother, wondering if it were possible Jack had given up on him and had left town.

He had to depend on Willa for directions and she led the way with confidence as she navigated the streets and alleys.

He tried not to think about what they would do if Jack never called the cell phone, if he was never able to mentally connect with his brother.

It was nearly dusk when they finally made it to the hospital, where Willa led him around to the back of the large brick building.

There was a back door and a parking lot that was filled with cars, but at the end of the building a small sidewalk led to a door nearly hidden by overgrown shrubs.

As Willa said, the door had a keypad and she quickly punched in a series of numbers and pulled on the handle. They expelled sighs of relief as the door opened.

Willa flipped the light switch on the wall and they entered a small room that held shelving on three walls. The shelves were empty and the room held the faint lingering scent of antiseptic hand soap and cleaning supplies.

The interior door of the room was closed and Jared hoped it would stay that way, that everyone in the hospital had forgotten about this old storage room in an equally old wing of the building. As Willa sank to the floor, he sat next to her. With his back against the wall he threw an arm around her shoulder and pulled her closer to him.

He had no words to comfort her, no thoughts to share that might make her feel that somehow this was all going to turn out okay.

"How did they find us?" she asked.

"Who knows? I don't have any idea how many men Kenneth might have working for him. There's no way to know how widespread they are around the city. It's possible one of them saw me at the fast-food stand and followed me back to the motel."

She shook her head and leaned back. "I made a phone call." Her features twisted with guilt. "Maybe that's how they tracked us."

"Who did you call?" he asked.

"Sunday night I called my friend at the hospital to tell her I was taking some time off. I was afraid if I didn't show up at work without an explanation then things would spin out of control. I'm sorry, Jared, it's probably my fault."

"No, it's not," he quickly said. "You did what you thought was best. Besides, for all we know Kenneth implanted some sort of tracking device inside me." A wealth of anger surged inside him. "I was nothing more than a lab animal to him."

"But that's not what you are," she protested. "That's not *who* you are." She leaned back against him once again. "That's just something terrible that happened to you, but you still have a whole future ahead of you and how you live that will discern what kind of a man you are."

"I want to be the kind of man you need. Willa, I am sorry that I involved you in this. If I'd known that night in the hospital how this was all going to play out I would have let Kenneth take me rather than put you at risk." He tightened his arm around her.

She tilted her head and smiled up at him. "I wouldn't have missed it all for the world," she replied. "I've lived my life pretty safe up until now. I've never taken any real chances, never put myself on the line for anything. Of course, it would really be nice if you could work up some kind of a happy ending in all this."

"I'm working on it," he said and was grateful she couldn't read his mind because no matter how he twisted things in his head he didn't see a happy ending in sight.

THERE WAS A BATHROOM down the hall outside of the storage room where they could get water to drink using the glass Jared had snatched from the bathroom sink in the motel as they went out the window. They tried to make as few trips as possible, knowing that each time they left the storage room they ran the risk of discovery.

When darkness began to fall, Willa turned out the light in the room, afraid that somebody might see it seeping out beneath the door and step inside to investigate.

As the hours passed she remained in Jared's arms, her head resting against his chest where she could hear the strong, steady beat of his heart. They talked in soft whispers.

He encouraged her to talk about her childhood, about the normal things that children did with their parents, experiences shared with family.

"Jack and I used to make things up about how we'd grow up if our parents hadn't died and Uncle Kenny hadn't adopted us," he said.

"Like what?" she asked and sensed a smile on his face.

"Well, it was obvious the father we conjured up between the two of us couldn't have had a job because he was too busy playing ball, going fishing and spending every minute of each day with us."

"And what about your mother?"

"She cooked only our favorite foods and never made us do chores. She was the most beautiful woman on the block and all of our friends wanted to hang out at our house." He laughed then, a low chuckle that had a bittersweet yearning.

"Maybe that's the way it would have been," she said softly, wishing she could give him all that had been stolen from him.

"I like to think so," he replied. "That one memory we had of our parents was such a happy one." He stiffened suddenly.

"What's wrong?" she asked, wondering if somehow Kenneth had found them yet again.

"I'm tapping in to that man's thoughts again—the one who was worried about his pregnant wife. He's worried about us, he's worrying that we're in trouble."

"Are you sure it isn't your brother's thoughts?"

"No, it's not Jack. It's hard to explain but the thoughts I get have a personality of their own, kind of like a color."

She tilted her head upward to look at him even though his features were barely discernable in the faint red exit light above the door. "Tell me about the colors." She wanted him to talk about anything but their circumstances, about what might happen when morning came.

He shifted positions and stretched his legs out before him without loosening his arm around her. "Good thoughts float through my head on a white mist. Bad thoughts are dark and tinged with red. Each one is just a little bit different and if I hear them often enough from the same person I can identify them. Jack's thoughts are white with a touch of blue."

"And what about my thoughts?" she asked.

"White with swirls of purple. They're always beautiful and they stir my passion. When I imagined what it would be like to find love, to make love, I never dreamed it would be as wonderful as it is."

In the darkness with nothing else on her mind, for the first time she processed that she was Jared's first, his only lover. The reality of that hadn't hit her until this very moment and now it struck her like a fatal impact with her past.

It was an unpleasant déjà vu as she realized how much Jared and Paul had in common. She had been Paul's first girlfriend, his first kiss and lover and at a time when she'd believed he would propose to her, he'd instead told her that he needed to go out and experience something new, something different.

How could Jared know he loved her if he had no experience in the arena of relationships, of love? To him, she'd been a voice in the darkness, but now he was no longer in the dark.

If he survived this, he had a whole new world of experiences waiting for him. It would be the height of selfishness, the pinnacle of cruelty to bind him to her when he was really at the very beginning of his life.

How long would it take before he realized what he felt for her was gratitude? How long before he hungered for new experiences and something more than a simple nurse who he'd thought he loved when he had nothing else to compare her to?

"Willa? Are you asleep?" he asked softly.

She didn't reply. She didn't want him to hear the emotion in her voice, the tears that weighed heavy in her heart, in her soul.

It had been unrealistic of her to visualize a future with him. How could he have a future when he didn't have a past?

She'd been with a man who had no real past when it came to love and it had ended badly. She didn't want to risk it again. Jared needed to build a past for himself before he could really create a future.

Squeezing her eyes tightly closed she realized that one way or another she was going to have to tell him goodbye.

He must have fallen asleep for the tension in his body eased and his breathing became slower and more regular. She stayed awake, simply loving the man he might have been, the man he had become and the one he would be.

He sat up suddenly and grabbed the phone as Willa's heart thrummed an anxious rhythm. "Yeah," he said, then closed his eyes as if overcome with emotion. "We're okay, Jack," he said. "Yeah, hang on."

To Willa's surprise he passed the phone to her. "Hello?" she whispered, afraid that it might be a friend calling to check in with her.

"Where's the best place for a pickup?" The voice was Jared's and yet not his. Jack.

"At the back of the emergency-room parking lot," she replied after a moment of thought.

"Which hospital?"

"Grand Forks Memorial," she said.

"Fifteen minutes." The line went dead.

"He'll be here in fifteen minutes," she said to Jared as she moved away from him.

"It's over." His voice trembled with emotion. He got to his feet and pulled her against his chest. "Everything is going to be fine now."

Before she could say anything he stepped out of the embrace and instead grabbed her hand and pulled her toward the door.

Night had fallen and as they left the storage

room Willa felt his excitement radiating through his hand into hers.

Although she was happy that he would soon be united with his brother, that within hours they would be away from Grand Forks and someplace where Kenneth couldn't hurt them anymore, her heart still ached because she knew for her this was the end of the story.

The night air was cool as Willa led him to the outer edges of the hospital property and around the building toward the emergency-room entrance.

They found a place to sit beneath a large tree at the very edges of the parking lot where the splash of the security lights didn't quite reach. From this vantage point they could see the cars coming and going from the parking lot.

"I feel like I'm about to be handed a life," Jared said, his voice a husky whisper.

"And it's going to be a wonderful life, filled with new experiences and people," Willa replied.

"All I care about is that you and I are together." His electric-blue eyes glowed in the semidarkness as he looked at her.

Willa stared back at him, loving the strong lines of his face, the sensual lips that created such magic when they touched hers. She loved him with all her heart and soul but now she had to figure out the easiest way to tell him goodbye.

Chapter Eleven

"I hear him now," Jared said, emotion thick in his voice. He closed his eyes and smiled. "It's like having part of my soul restored to have his thoughts inside my head again."

Jared got to his feet and pulled up Willa, as well. He kept his gaze focused on the entrance, waiting for his twin brother to arrive as Willa fought back tears.

As a dark sedan entered the lot Jared tightened his fingers around Willa's. They would not leave the cover of the trees and the darkness unless they were sure that it was Jack and not some other danger that had finally arrived.

The car drove slowly toward them and when it reached the last row of cars it stopped and the passenger door opened.

Jack got out.

Jared released Willa's hands and ran toward his twin. As the two men embraced tears escaped

Willa's eyes. These were tears of happiness for the two men who had been ripped apart from each other and now were finally reunited.

Jack looked exactly like Jared except he was heavier and his dark hair was longer. When the two finally broke their embrace, Jared turned to where Willa still stood in the shadows of the trees.

"Willa?"

She quickly swiped the tears from her cheeks and went to join them. Jared made introductions and Jack took her hand in his.

"Thank you for helping my brother," he said, his deep voice almost the exact timbre of Jared's. "I'm forever in your debt for everything you've done for him."

"She's coming with us," Jared said.

Jack looked at Jared in surprise and he must have seen something in his brother's eyes, on Jared's face, that told him how important Willa was to him. "Okay, then let's go before we attract too much attention out here."

"I'm not going." The words were laced with pain as they fell from Willa's lips.

Jared looked at her in stunned surprise. "What do you mean?"

She shook her head, digging inside to find the strength she needed. "I'm staying here, Jared. I'm not going with you and your brother."

Jack stepped back from the two of them. "Settle whatever you need to, but make it fast." He got back into the car, leaving the two of them alone.

Jared stared at her, his eyes filled with questions. He reached for her hands but she kept her arms tightly at her sides, afraid that if he touched her she'd change her mind.

"Willa, what's going on? I thought we were doing this together, that we were going to be together. I love you and I thought you loved me." His eyes were shadowed with pain and confusion.

"I got caught up in the moment," she said as she took a step back from him. "And I think if you look deep in your heart you'll realize you did the same thing."

He lunged toward her and gripped her shoulders, his eyes blazing with need. "I know what I want, I know what I feel. I love you, Willa, and I want to spend the rest of my life with you. Don't be afraid. We'll get the future we talked about, with children and a dog and a house."

Each of his words were like arrows slicing through the very heart of her. She wanted to fall into his arms, to tell him she'd go with him anywhere, but she knew she couldn't do that. Better to hurt now than continue to love deeper, more profoundly, and then have him realize he wanted something different, something more.

"I'm not afraid, Jared," she finally replied. "I've just realized I'm not in love with you." *Washington, Adams, Jefferson, Madison...* she filled her head with the names, hoping it would block him from reading her mind, from knowing her true feelings for him.

He held tight to her shoulders for a long moment and then dropped his arms to his sides, his eyes less bright, more hollow as he continued to stare at her.

"I don't know what's going through your mind, but I know one thing for certain. You love me, Willa, and we belong together. I can't force you to go with us, nor would I want to, but be sure this is what you want to do, that you really want to let me, let us go."

She drew in a deep breath in an attempt to halt the tears that burned hot behind her eyes. She didn't want to cry in front of him. She didn't want him to see her pain, to know how difficult this was for her. Wrapping her arms around herself, she took a step back from him. "I'm sure."

For one long agonizing moment their gazes remained locked. Willa continued to block him although she was dying inside.

"Have a wonderful life, Jared," she finally said and then turned and walked back to the shadows beneath the tree.

"Willa, if you ever need me, all you have to do is think of me and I'll find you." He turned and walked to the car. When he reached the back door he turned and looked in her direction one last time. In the light of the parking lot she could see the sadness, the torture that twisted his features.

She held in her tears until he disappeared into the backseat of the car and it pulled out of the parking lot. Only then did she sink to her knees in the cool grass and weep for all that might have been.

JARED FELT NUMB. As he sat in the backseat behind a man he didn't know and they pulled away from the hospital he felt as if the bad dream that had been his life so far continued.

How had he lost the most important piece of his heart? He and Willa had spent the hours in the storage room talking about their future, sharing little pieces of their pasts. Had the love he'd felt from her really been nothing more than an illusion? Was it as she'd said, that she'd simply gotten caught up in the moment and had mistaken her feelings for love?

She had absolutely blindsided him. He'd never seen this coming, had never guessed that he would be in a car driving away from her.

"You okay?" Jack turned in the seat and looked back at him.

Jared tried to shove thoughts of Willa out of his mind, knowing his brother needed to know what had happened since the moment Kenneth had taken them out of Willa's house.

He was introduced to the driver of the car, Zack O'Hara, an FBI agent who explained that he was stationed outside of Washington, D.C., but was working the case to arrest Kenneth.

By the time they pulled up in front of the doors of a nice hotel, Jared had told them about being held captive in the old psychiatric hospital, about the injection he'd been given and their escape from the premises.

Jack and Jared got out and Zack drove off to park the car. "Let's head up to the room. There are people you need to meet," Jack said.

As they waited for the elevator Jack quickly filled him in on what had happened in his life for the past six months.

He'd been found running through the woods in Rapid City, South Dakota, by Claudia Reynolds. He'd passed out in front of her car and she'd taken him home with her. It didn't take long for them both to realize he was suffering from some form of amnesia.

Over the next couple of weeks Jack slowly began to get some memories back. When he and Claudia were attacked by Red, he managed to incapacitate the man but before they could get him to the proper authorities he took his own life.

Red's death had alerted the FBI, which had been looking for him in connection with some recent abductions. Finally, Jack remembered the existence of his brother and had been working ever since to find Jared.

Jack assured Jared that it was no longer just the two of them trying to take down Kenneth. Jack had connected with many of the men and women who had managed to escape from Kenneth or had been let go, and together with the FBI they wouldn't rest until Kenneth was behind bars.

"I don't think he'll leave town for at least another couple of days," Jared said as they got into the elevator that would take them up to the suite. "He knows I'm still here and he wants me back in his clutches."

"What about Willa? Will he try to use her to get to you?" Jack asked.

Pain filled Jared's chest as he thought of her. "I don't think so," he replied. He told Jack about encountering the lab rat at Willa's house. "I think both Willa and I made it clear that she was nothing but a tool I'd used to get out of the hospital and I had no intention of telling her any of my secrets or plans."

The two fell silent as the elevator door opened

and Jack led Jared down a long corridor to the last room. He used a key card to open the door and they stepped into the suite.

One man and three women sat at the large dining table in the main area. All of them jumped up from their chairs as they entered.

One woman rushed toward him and gave him a hug. "Oh, Jared, you have no idea what having you back means to your brother," she exclaimed as she stepped away from him.

He realized this must be Claudia, the woman his brother loved, the woman his brother had married several weeks before. He looked over at Jack and then back to Claudia, emotion thick in his chest. "It's like a dream come true for me," he replied.

He didn't want to think about all the other dreams that had shattered into pieces when Willa had refused to come with him. He'd think about it later, when he was all alone.

Jack introduced the others and by that time Zack had returned to the room. Jared took a seat across from the man who had been introduced as Drew. "It's you," he said suddenly. "It's your thoughts I've been picking up over the past day or two."

Drew leaned back in his chair and eyed Jared in surprise. "Why would you be picking up my thoughts instead of anyone else's?"

"You were part of the experiments, right?"

Jared asked and Drew nodded. "What ability did you acquire?"

Drew pulled a small army knife from his pocket and opened the blade. Before Jared realized what he was about to do, he ran the blade across the back of his hand. Jared gasped and watched as blood welled to the surface of the wound. Almost immediately the wound began to close and within minutes it was as if it had never existed.

"He must have injected me with some component of your blood," Jared said thoughtfully as he remembered the way his own wounds had healed.

"Now let's talk about the important things," Zack said. "Like where we can find Kenneth."

"There's no question in my mind that he's still here in town," Jared said. "As long as he thinks I'm still here, he won't leave. He will want samples from me since he gave me that injection of Drew's blood."

"Then the goal is for us to find him before he leaves town," Zack exclaimed. "We have to get him into custody and find out about his foreign contacts before he can get that research overseas. He has to be brought in and he has to be brought in alive."

For the next two hours they all talked about Kenneth and what was being done to find him in Grand Forks. It didn't take long for Jared to learn the personalities of the people in the room.

Zack was a take-charge kind of man and his scientist fiancée, Kendra, was quiet but intelligent. Drew had the inquisitive mind of the reporter he was and his pregnant wife, Melinda, seemed caring and sweet.

It wasn't lost on Jared that all the men had found significant others despite their pasts, despite everything that had happened to each of them. *Willa.* His heart cried in pain with each and every thought of her.

Dinner was ordered in and after eating, they drifted into their respective rooms. Jack provided a pillow and a blanket for Jared to sleep on the sofa.

"You going to be okay?" Jack asked once the others had left the room.

Jared hesitated a moment and then nodded. "I'll be better when I know that Uncle Ken is in a place where he can never hurt anyone again."

Jack smiled. "I wasn't asking you about that. I was asking about her. I feel your pain, bro, and I wish I could do something to help ease it."

Jared released a ragged sigh. "I don't think anything or anyone can help ease it. I love her, Jack. I know it sounds crazy, but I am so in love with her."

Jack placed his hand on Jared's shoulder. "It doesn't sound crazy to me. It doesn't take long to know when it's right."

Racing a hand through his hair, Jared looked at

his brother. "It felt right. I know it was right. But if that's the truth then why am I here alone?"

"Maybe she just couldn't handle everything. I mean, we don't exactly come without baggage."

Jared shook his head. "I just don't believe that. She was amazingly strong and courageous and she stood side by side with me when we thought the potential outcome might be death. Why would she turn her back on me now when we were finally out of danger?"

"I can't answer that," Jack replied.

"Yeah, neither can I." He forced a smile at his brother. "Go to bed. I'll be fine. Nursing a broken heart is just a new experience, that's all."

The two said good-night and Jared found himself alone in the room. He walked over to the window that looked out on the parking lot below.

Willa? Why?

His heart squeezed painfully tight in his chest as he thought of her. It had been right, the two of them had been right together. Fate had put him in her hospital and it had been her spirit that had pulled him through the darkness, that had given him a reason to live. Dammit, they belonged together.

Willa? Where are you? Why aren't you here with me? Can you feel my love in your thoughts, can you feel it in the depths of your soul? Talk to me, Willa. Just let me know you're there.

He emptied his head of all thoughts, hoping to hear her voice inside him, waiting to feel that connection with her.

But there was nothing.

Chapter Twelve

"You still aren't going to tell me what happened?" Nancy asked three nights after Willa had watched Jared leave with his brother. "It's obvious that you're upset and I can't help you if I don't know what you're upset about."

The two women were on a break and seated in the nurses' lounge. Willa hadn't gone home after Jared had left. Instead she'd called Nancy and asked if she could stay with her for a couple of days.

"If I told you what's happened you'd think I needed mental help," Willa replied. It was all too outlandish to try to explain—a crazy scientist, a handsome test subject and a run for their lives. Who would believe it? "However, you'll be happy to know that I've decided to go home tonight after work. I've been enough of a burden on you."

Nancy waved a hand dismissively. "You haven't been a burden. In fact I've enjoyed your company."

"Thanks, but it's time I go home." She'd been afraid of going back to the house since leaving Jared, but she realized eventually she'd have to return. She told herself that Kenneth Sykes could have no interest in her, that there was no danger to her since Jared had escaped.

Besides, by now Kenneth had probably left town. With Jared gone there was no reason for him to hang around here in Grand Forks.

"Back to work," Willa now said as she checked her watch.

"You sure you don't want to stay at my place for another couple of days?" Nancy asked.

Willa smiled and shook her head. "Thanks, Nancy. You've been a good friend, but it's time I get back to my own place now." Willa knew that the longer she put it off the more difficult it would be to leave Nancy's homey apartment.

"Then I guess I'll drop you at your place when we leave here this evening," Nancy said.

"I'd appreciate it. Since we're both off tomorrow I'll plan on coming by sometime in the morning to get the few things I have at your place," Willa said as the two left the lounge.

"That's fine. I'm not planning on going anywhere tomorrow," Nancy replied.

The two women parted ways in the corridor and Willa headed for her station. As always she tried to keep her mind as full as possible with patient information, errands that needed to be run and useless minutia that would keep thoughts of Jared at bay.

Her heart had been rent in half and she felt as if it would never be healed again. Allowing Jared to drive away in that car had been the most difficult thing she'd ever done in her entire life. But even now, despite the pain, she felt that she'd done the right thing.

The worst part of it all was that just before she fell asleep each night she thought she heard Jared calling to her and she heard the heartbreak in his voice, felt it resonating deep inside her. And each night before she went to sleep she blocked her brain, thinking of dead presidents so he wouldn't hear her longing for him.

She'd thought she'd known heartbreak when Paul had broken up with her. She'd believed she'd known loneliness in the days and months after he'd been gone from her life. But it had been nothing compared to the pain and loneliness she felt now without Jared.

The rest of her shift seemed to last forever but finally it was time for her to go home—back to the house where she'd found not only danger, but also love.

She met Nancy by the parking-lot door and together the two went out into the cool evening late

April air. "Before you know it summer will be here," Nancy said.

Where would Jared be when summer arrived? Would he be on a beach somewhere with his brother? Would they even remain in the United States? Willa shook her head to dislodge these thoughts.

"You sure you're okay with going home?" Nancy asked as they got into her car. "Even though you won't tell me what happened to you while you were gone from the hospital, it's obvious to me that you've been afraid to go home."

"I just needed a couple of days with a friend," Willa replied, "but I'm okay now."

She told herself she was okay once again as Nancy pulled up in her driveway and she got out of the car. She gave Nancy a cheerful wave and then turned and faced the house.

The last time she'd been inside had been to retrieve the cell phone and Jared had screamed in her head to get out. There was no Jared now to tell her if danger was inside, there was only her own intuition to rely on.

She left the driveway and walked around to the back of the house. She still had the key to the back door from when she'd gone inside before and as she approached it she looked around the area to see if there was anything to cause her alarm.

The neighborhood was quiet and she saw nobody

hiding behind the bushes or lurking in the shadows. Drawing in a deep breath, she unlocked the back door and shoved it open. She took a tentative step into the kitchen and felt herself begin to relax.

Nobody jumped out of the cabinets or barreled in from the living room. The only sounds were the normal ones the house usually made, the hum of the refrigerator and the ticking of the clock hanging on the wall.

She tried not to remember Jared sitting at her kitchen table, tried desperately to forget the way he'd filled the room with his presence.

He's gone, she reminded herself, and hopefully he was finally going to get to experience life the way he was meant to. He would meet women and date and eventually fall in love and probably forget that he ever knew and believed himself in love with a nurse named Willa.

She'd thought all her tears had been spent but she'd been wrong. She sank to the table as her vision blurred with a fresh burst of tears.

It was ridiculous to be crying so hard over a man she'd known for just a little over a week. She hadn't cried half this hard when she and Paul had broken up and she'd been dating him for years.

But this was different. Despite the fact that she'd known Jared only a short period of time she knew him on a level she'd never known Paul.

Jared had been inside her head, he'd shared her thoughts, her dreams, and he'd shared his own with her. He'd invaded her dreams and had made her feel like the most special woman on the face of the earth.

For the first time since she'd shoved him away regret niggled at her soul. Maybe she should have given them a chance. Maybe she'd been so worried about being hurt later that she'd inflicted hurt on them both too quickly.

It didn't matter now. He was gone and she had no idea where his brother lived. She had a feeling Jack wasn't in any phone book. He'd escaped from Sykes the same night that Jared had and while Jared had been in his coma Jack had probably been flying under the radar to build some semblance of a life for himself.

She hoped that together they could do something to stop Kenneth. What he'd done to Jack and Jared had been criminal and if what Jared had told her was true and Kenneth was abducting children to use in his experiments then it was nothing short of monstrous.

She wept until her nose was stuffed and her tears were spent, then roused herself from the table with a weariness that had been with her since the night in the parking lot when she'd watched Jack's car drive away.

Knowing she should fix herself something for supper even though she wasn't a bit hungry, she opened the freezer and stared at the contents, trying to forget what it had felt like to be in Jared's arms, to have his lips against hers, to feel his love wrapped around her so tight that there was no room for anything else.

She slammed the freezer door, deciding there was no way she could eat a bite. Maybe she'd feel better after a long hot shower.

As she walked through the living room and down the hallway she turned on lights to ward off the darkness of night. Any fear that she might have felt in coming back here was gone, replaced by the familiar weariness that weighed on her like a thousand pounds resting on her shoulders.

It was too late for regrets, too late to change anything. All she could do was somehow manage to get on with her life. She had her work at the hospital and for now that had to be enough.

She walked into her bedroom and turned on the light and a scream rose to the back of her throat as she saw Kenneth sitting on the edge of her bed.

"Hello, Willa," he said with a pleasant smile. "We've been waiting for you." He gestured toward the corner where a big-shouldered blond man stood at attention.

She froze for a moment as terror shot through

her. Acting purely on instinct, she whirled on her heels and raced down the hallway, but before she could reach the front door the big man grabbed her beneath her arms and physically picked her up.

She kicked and punched as he carried her to the living room. He threw her on the sofa and pulled a gun as Kenneth came into the room with a syringe in one hand.

"What's that?" she asked in horror as she stared at the syringe. *Jared, I'm in trouble. He's here.*

"A little something to help you answer my questions," Kenneth replied. "I need to know where Jared is."

"I don't know," she replied. "I have no idea where he is and even if you give me that shot the answer is going to be the same." *Help me, somebody please help me.* The words thundered in her head as Kenneth moved closer.

FOR THE PAST THREE DAYS Jared had been catching up with everything that had happened since the night he'd left The Facility and wound up in the coma.

Jack told him that a dead woman had been found in one of the freezers at The Facility. It appeared that she'd been pregnant at the time of her death and the unborn baby had been removed.

Drew told him that dead woman had been his

former girlfriend and he believed that the baby she'd carried had been his. They all assumed that Kenneth was eager to find out what would happen if his test subjects had children, wondered how his experiments affected the offspring.

They all had remained in the hotel in Grand Forks, believing that Kenneth was still in town. The FBI, in an effort to locate the man, was checking the airport and bus travel and had set up checkpoints on the roads for people leaving town by car.

Nobody wanted him to slip away again, afraid that he would manage to get out of the country and take his research with him. It had become an issue of national security.

Jack also told Jared about a rancher named Matt Whitlock and a woman named Shelley who'd had their four-year-old son, Trevor, kidnapped by Kenneth. Matt was another of Kenneth's experiments and he and Shelley had worked together and used their abilities to find Trevor and get him back safely with them. They were living a happy life on Matt's ranch in Colorado.

So many people, Jared now realized as he stood at the window where he'd spent much of his time over the past three days, so many people whose lives had been disrupted and forever changed by the machinations of Kenneth.

He and Jared had tried to figure out why they

hadn't been able to communicate with each other that well since the coma. The only thing they'd decided was perhaps it was because Willa had been so close to Jared, had filled his thoughts and his heart to the point that he hadn't been able to connect with Jack.

And as always, his thoughts returned to Willa. Since the moment the car had pulled away from the hospital and they'd left her standing in the parking lot Jared had played and replayed each and every moment they'd shared together in his head. He tried desperately to understand what had gone wrong. What had happened between her "I love you" and her goodbye?

No matter how many times he went over things, he couldn't find an answer; he couldn't find the reason why they weren't together at this moment.

"Jared, you need to eat something," Jack said from behind him.

"I'm not hungry." He left the window and instead sat on the sofa. The others were gathered around the table enjoying the pizza they'd carried in for the evening meal.

I'm worried about you. Jack's thought filled Jared's head.

Stop worrying. I'm just suffering a little heartbreak, that's all, Jared replied. *I'll be fine. I just need a little more time.*

Jack moved to the table and sat next to his wife as Jared leaned his head back and closed his eyes.

Funny, all he'd ever thought about when they'd been held captive was living a normal life. Heartbreak was part of a normal life, but in all his imaginings, he'd never envisioned how badly it would hurt.

Jared, I'm in trouble. He's here.

The thought thundered in his head—Willa's thought. He let out a loud gasp and shot up from the sofa. "Kenneth is at Willa's."

The others stared at him for a long moment, their expressions ranging from disbelief to stunned surprise. "Are you sure?" Jack asked.

Jared nodded, a sense of urgency filling his veins. "She's in trouble. We have to go."

The men all jumped out of their chairs. "I'll get the car and meet you in the front," Zack said as he flew out of the room.

Jack grabbed hold of Jared's shoulder. "What do you hear, Jared?"

"She's calling for me. Kenneth is with her and she's terrified. Oh, God, her fear is enormous." Emotion pressed tight against his chest, nearly suffocating him as he felt her terror.

"Let's go," Jack said and together he, Jared and Drew hurried out of the room and down the hallway to the elevator.

"I thought he'd leave her alone," Jared said half in anger, half in self-recrimination. "I thought she was out of danger." Guilt stabbed him like an arrow through his chest.

He couldn't wait another minute for the elevator. He shoved through the door that led to the stairs and raced down them, his heart pounding as he realized he could no longer hear Willa's thoughts.

Had Kenneth killed her? Why? Why would he have gone after her? Surely Willa had told him she didn't know where Jared had gone after they'd parted ways.

Surely he wouldn't hurt her, he tried to tell himself, but then he thought of that poor woman's lifeless body stuffed in a freezer and he knew that human life held no value to a man like Kenneth.

He was vaguely aware of the thundering footsteps of Jack and Drew just behind him as he finally reached the first floor. He shoved open the door that led to the lobby and raced toward the front door.

Hang on, Willa. I'm coming!

Within seconds the four of them were in the car and headed toward Willa's place. Jared's stomach clenched with knots of tension as he mentally urged Zack to drive faster.

"I've got a couple of agents meeting us a block from Willa's house. We have to make a plan," Zack said as he fishtailed around a corner. "We can't just barge in not knowing what's going on inside. The last thing we want is to bring more danger to Willa."

"And we have to make sure we get Kenneth alive," Drew reminded them. "We need to know his foreign contacts and make sure none of this research has already gone someplace else."

Jared didn't care about research or foreign contacts; all he cared about was Willa. He knew it was possible Kenneth would kill her just because he could, just to prove a point to Jared. And if that happened, Jared would kill the man with his bare hands.

The drive seemed to take forever, as each minute ticked by in agonizing slowness. And with each minute he tried to contact her, using all his mental abilities to attempt to reach her.

There was no reply, nothing, and that scared him more than anything.

There was little talk until they reached a car parked against the curb a block away from Willa's house. Two men stood by the car and Zack got out and spoke to them briefly, then returned to the car.

"We'll go on foot from here," he said.

They all got out of the car and Zack quickly introduced them to Agents Taylor and Mack. "Jared, you know the layout of the house. Anything special we need to know about?" Agent Mack asked. He was a big man, with intelligent brown eyes and stern features that looked as if they'd never held a smile.

"No, nothing special," Jared replied. Except the woman he loved was inside with a madman, he thought in desperation.

"Mack and I will take the back," Agent Taylor said. "Zack, you go to the left side of the house and Drew will take the right. Jared, you see if you can get a glimpse through the front window. We don't need any heroes here. We'll assess the scene before making any moves."

"We're wasting time," Jared said impatiently. He couldn't stand it any longer. He felt as if he were suffocating, as if his blood was boiling with the need to act. He took off down the street, aware of the others following closely behind him.

Darkness had fallen and the men moved like silent shadows toward Willa's house. Jared's heart beat so fast it was a wonder all the neighbors didn't hear it resonating in the air.

Please don't let us be too late, his heart cried out. *Even if I can't have her with me every day for the rest of my life, please let me get there to save her life.* But the silence in his head was deafening and he feared that they were, indeed, too late.

Chapter Thirteen

Mindless.

That was the way Willa felt as she sat on the sofa and stared at Kenneth. She had no idea what had been in the injection he'd given her, but it hadn't just made her drowsy, it had filled her with a strange sense of well-being.

Someplace in the very deepest recesses of her mind she knew she was in trouble, but she felt nothing but a curious numbness.

"Now, I'm going to ask you again," Kenneth said. "Where is Jared?"

"I already told you, I don't know. I left him." She fought against a yawn. She knew she should be afraid, that there was no way Kenneth was going to walk away and leave her alive, but the drug had a hold on her and she simply couldn't summon any reasonable sense of fear.

"You left him where?" Kenneth asked.

"Jack picked him up in the hospital parking lot," she replied.

Kenneth's eyes narrowed. "Jack? He's here in town?"

She nodded. "He and Jared are together now. You couldn't stop their reunion."

"And where were they going, Willa?"

"I don't know. I didn't want to know." Suddenly she was overwhelmed with sadness. "He wanted me to go with them. He loves me and I love him, but I couldn't go. I knew he needed to experience life without me."

"A touching tale," Kenneth said, the coldness in his voice seeping into Willa's veins and shooting a chill through her. "Did either of them mention where Jack has been living? Where they might be going from here?"

"I don't know. Don't you understand? He didn't tell me anything about where they were going." She just wanted them to go away; she wanted the mad scientist and his henchman gone so she could just go to sleep and dream of Jared. "I can't tell you anything," she said wearily. "I just can't tell you what I don't know."

"We're getting nowhere here," Kenneth said in obvious disgust. "I think that our lovely nurse has outlived her usefulness," he said to White.

His words penetrated the fog that had been in

Willa's head. Horror stabbed through her as she realized she was about to be killed. She watched in stunned silence as White pulled his gun from the front of his pants where he'd tucked it during the questioning.

Jared!

She cried his name in her head, in her heart as the barrel of the gun was pointed at her.

At that moment the house seemed to explode. Willa screamed as the front window burst inward and Jared dived through. His body flew between White and Willa, and he caught a bullet in his shoulder that had been intended for her. Willa screamed again as Jared crumbled to the floor.

Another man stepped in from the kitchen and pointed his gun at White. "Drop your weapon," he yelled. "Drop it now!"

White held his gaze for a long moment and then put his gun into his mouth and pulled the trigger. As he slumped to the ground Willa slid off the sofa and crawled to Jared, who was on the floor holding his shoulder.

"Don't move," Jack yelled at Kenneth, who remained standing in the middle of the living-room floor.

Willa pressed her hand against Jared's wound, weeping uncontrollably. "Don't you die, Jared. I love you. I love you and I don't want to lose you."

"It's okay," he said as he sat up and pulled her against him with his good arm. "It's going to be all right. I can feel it healing right now."

"So the injection is doing what it was supposed to do," Kenneth said, a note of triumph in his voice.

There was a moment of silence and then a small pop sounded from someplace outside and the front of Kenneth's shirt exploded in scarlet blood. His eyes widened and he opened his mouth as if to speak, then fell forward to the floor.

Jack rushed to him and pressed his fingers against his neck, then shook his head. "Dammit, he's dead."

"Who fired that shot?" one of the men demanded. He looked around the room at all the men who were there, then flew out the front door.

Willa didn't care who had killed Kenneth, she didn't care about White committing suicide, all she cared about was the man who helped her up off the floor and onto the sofa.

"You're safe now," he said. "You never have to be afraid again."

"You need a doctor?" Jack asked.

Jared shook his head. "I'm fine. Take care of whatever you need to do. I'm staying right here." He tightened his arms around Willa.

She looked up at him, finding it hard to believe that he was here with her, that Kenneth was gone and could never hurt them again. "He gave me a shot," she said groggily. "It was some kind of truth serum. He asked me where you were, where your brother was staying, but I couldn't tell him what he wanted to know."

"Can you tell me what I need to know?" Jared asked as he swept a stand of hair from her cheek.

She looked into his beautiful blue eyes and knew what he wanted to hear, what he needed to know. "I love you," she whispered softly, "and that's why I have to let you go." She drew a tremulous breath, closed her eyes and knew no more.

She awoke in her own bed with the morning sun at the window and Jared spooned around her back. For a long moment she remained unmoving, bathed in his body heat and reluctant to face what lay ahead.

More goodbyes. That was what the day would hold. Once again she would have to tell Jared goodbye. But at least this time she would know that he wasn't looking over his shoulder for Kenneth. She would have the comfort in knowing that not only was she safe from Kenneth, but Jared also was.

With a deep sigh she slid from the bed, grateful that she didn't awaken Jared. She wasn't eager for the new goodbyes to begin. She didn't need to bother with a robe; she was still clad in the scrubs that she'd worn the day before.

The events of the previous night were a jumble

in her mind. Whatever drug Kenneth had given her had not only fogged her brain, but had also eventually knocked her out cold. She was surprised to find that the broken living-room window had been boarded up sometime during the night and the blood from the wounded and dead had been washed away.

Thank God Jared had heard her cries for help. Thank God he'd still been in the town of Grand Forks and had been able to respond. Otherwise it would have been her blood that somebody would have been cleaning up this morning.

"I woke up and you were gone."

She turned to see Jared. Clad only in a pair of jeans and with his hair tousled, his natural sexiness nearly stole her breath. "I see your shoulder is healed," she said.

He raised his arm. "Almost as good as new. Amazing, isn't it?" His lips curved into a smile that shot straight into her heart.

She nodded and wrapped her arms around her waist, as if to form a defense against him. Even though Kenneth was dead nothing had really changed between her and Jared. "Who killed Kenneth?" she asked.

The smile on his face fell and he shook his head. "We don't know. The shot came from outside but all our men were accounted for inside the house.

We wanted him alive and the FBI is doing their best to figure out who shot him and why."

"I can't say I'm sorry he's dead and that his research died with him," she replied.

"That's just it, we don't know if his research died with him. But I don't want to talk about him. I want to talk about us." He took several steps toward her.

"There is no us," she replied painfully. "Jared, I'm grateful you all showed up last night. Thank God you heard me crying out to you. You saved my life, but nothing has changed for you and me."

"That's not true. I now know for sure that you love me and that changes everything," he said, his soft voice like a warm caress upon her heart.

She steeled herself against it, against him. *Remember Paul,* she told herself. *It would be like the past all over again.*

"I'm not Paul," he said.

"Get out of my head!" She pressed her hands on her ears, as if to block his entrance into her brain.

"I'm not in your head, Willa. I'm in your heart." He moved closer to her and pulled her hands down, then held tight to them. "Willa, I'm not Paul," he repeated. "I'm much luckier than Paul. He didn't know what he wanted, but I do."

She pulled her hands from his. "How can you know what you want? You haven't had any life experiences. You haven't been with any other woman besides me."

He released a small sigh. "Willa, I imagine there are lots of people in this world who have only had one lover. There are high-school sweethearts who live happily ever after, there are people who fall in love with the first man or woman they date. Would you discount their love because they don't have more experience? I had lots of nurses taking care of me when I was in the coma. I was in their heads, privy to their thoughts, but it was you I fell in love with long before I regained consciousness. When it's right, Willa, there's no need to look further. It just wasn't right for you and Paul, but we're right."

I love you and you love me. Give us a chance, Willa. Don't throw away what we have.

"Willa, it takes some people a lifetime to find what we already have," he continued. "When I've found what I want, when I have the very best, why on earth would I look for something different?"

She stared into his amazingly blue eyes and her love for him buoyed up inside her. There was more than a little truth in his words. She knew now that she and Paul hadn't been right. She'd never loved Paul like she loved Jared.

She reached out and touched his shoulder, where a pucker of skin was the only indication that there had been a wound. "You could have been killed."

"I would have gladly died to save your life." He reached up and stroked a finger down the side of her cheek. "For God's sake, Willa, at least let me walk away from all this with the girl."

She laughed and in that moment she knew she couldn't walk away from him a second time; she knew that she'd be a fool not to embrace what they had and run with it.

Sobering, she released a sigh. "I want you to experience everything that life has to offer, Jared."

"I want that, too, but only if you're by my side." He took her into his arms and this time she didn't fight him. "There are so many firsts we can experience together," he continued. "Like marriage and becoming parents and sushi."

Once again a bubble of laughter filled her. "Sushi?"

He grinned down at her. "I've always wondered about sushi." He sobered then. "We belong together, Willa. You're the only woman I want, the one who's perfect for me. Don't send me away again."

Certainly life wouldn't be completely normal with a man like Jared, but as far as Willa was concerned normal was vastly overrated. Besides, in his eyes she saw the kind of love she'd yearned for, the kind that would last a lifetime.

"What to try some sushi for dinner?" she asked.

His arms tightened around her. "We could always try it a month from now."

"Or a year, or ten years." Last night she hadn't believed she had a future and now it shimmered in front of her like a dazzling jewel.

As he captured her lips with his, she tasted his passion and his love for her and she knew he was the man who would share the rest of her life. Jared had walked right out of her dreams and into her heart and his lips tasted of forever.

Epilogue

Willa's backyard had been transformed into a park setting with picnic tables and benches and a grill sizzling with hamburgers and hot dogs.

It had been a little over a month since the night that Kenneth had been killed. The ensuing investigation had uncovered some startling results. The man who had shot Kenneth was Green, the last of the triplets who had been genetically enhanced to protect and serve Kenneth. Green had seen an opportunity to take over. He'd been working in consort with a drug lord in Central America who had been providing the funding for the entire operation.

Green had been Kenneth's ultimate experimental failure, a man who had rejected the change but had instead embraced his creator's thirst for power.

This would be the first time since that night that all the players who had been there were coming together again. Willa and Jared were hosting the barbecue and intended to announce their official engagement during the festivities.

She stood at the back door and watched Jared and Jack arguing good-naturedly over who would man the grill. As always her heart expanded in her chest as she looked at Jared.

The past month with him had been an amazing journey filled with love and laughter, but also a bit of uncertainty. Jared had no idea what he wanted to do with the rest of his life and Willa had encouraged him to take his time. She was still working at the hospital and made enough money to support them. Besides, she had no doubt that whatever he decided to do, he would be terrific at it.

"Anything I can do to help?" Claudia asked as she walked up to Willa.

"No, I think I have everything under control," Willa replied. "You need to sit down?"

Claudia placed a hand on her pregnant stomach. She and Jack had been delighted to discover she was carrying twins. "No, I'm fine. Ask me again in a couple of months when I'm too big to fit in a chair."

Willa laughed and then looked at Jack and Jared once again. "It's so good to see them together."

Claudia nodded. "Jack was missing a piece of himself before we found you and Jared. I knew that he'd never know real happiness unless he got closure where Jared was concerned."

"It's a shame Drew and Melinda couldn't be here," Willa said.

Claudia smiled. "Drew is so protective of Melinda he didn't want her traveling close to her due date."

"Jared sent his best wishes for the two of them via head-talking," Willa replied. "Since Jared got Drew's blood in whatever injection Kenneth gave him, Jared has been able to communicate with Drew."

"I know Zack has been trying to hunt down who had been funding Kenneth's research, but I can't help but be glad Kenneth is dead. What he did was atrocious."

"Did I hear my name?" Zack and Kendra joined Claudia and Willa.

"I was wondering how long it would take before you stepped into the fight for the grill tongs," Willa said.

Zack grinned and looked at Jack and Jared. "I'm not getting between those two." As they all watched Jared laughed and walked toward them, leaving Jack in charge of the fire.

"You know, it's possible I might be able to find a way to reverse what Kenneth did to you all," Kendra said.

Jared frowned thoughtfully and looked at Willa. "I don't know about you, Zack, or how Jack might feel about it, but this is who I am now." He looked at Willa once again. "But if you'd want me to do that, then I would."

Willa moved closer to him and smiled up at him. "I love you just the way you are. You don't have to change a thing as far as I'm concerned."

"Which brings me to the reason we've brought you all here," Jared said. "Jack, come here for a minute."

Jack left the grill and joined them as Jared fell to one knee. Willa's heart suddenly began to race as she realized what Jared was about to do.

Jared held her gaze as he reached into his pocket and removed a small velvet box. "Willa, I know we've talked about our future but I want to make it official. Will you marry me, Willa? Will you be my bride for the rest of our lives?"

"Yes, oh, yes," she exclaimed and her breath caught in her throat as he opened the box and took out the simple diamond ring and slid it on her finger.

As the others cheered and whooped, Jared rose and took Willa into his arms for a kiss that sealed their future. When he ended the kiss his eyes gleamed with pleasure.

"I have an engagement present to give you," he said.

"Oh, Jared, you've given me more than I ever dreamed possible," she protested.

"Ah, but this is something special." He walked over to the shed and opened the door and disappeared inside. Willa looked at the others curiously, but they all shrugged, except for Jack, who gave her a smile that let her know he was aware of the gift.

Jared walked out of the shed with a fat, golden puppy in his arms. The puppy licked the underside of his chin and then wiggled to get free. Willa laughed with abandon, her love for Jared filling her up.

He carried the puppy to her and grinned. "He doesn't have a name yet, but I've been assured he'll grow up to be fluffy and loving, just like the dog you always dreamed of owning."

At that moment the grill began to smoke and Jack raced back to make sure that nothing was burning as the puppy managed to get loose from Jared and became the center of attention.

The afternoon passed with good food and laughter. The puppy was so excited by everything and everyone he eventually fell asleep with his nose resting on Willa's sandal.

All too quickly it was time for goodbyes and promises to get together again soon. With the puppy locked into the kitchen by a gate across the doorway, Jared and Willa returned to the backyard to finish the last of the cleanup.

He picked up her hand, and the engagement ring sparkled in the last of the evening sun. "Do you like your ring?"

She smiled at him. "Jared, you could have given

me a plastic ring from a gumball machine and I would have loved it." She held her hand up. "I love it, and I love you."

"I'm glad you didn't want Kendra to try to reverse my abilities." He leaned closer to her and placed a hand on her stomach. "If I lost my ability then I wouldn't be able to communicate with the baby you're carrying."

Willa froze and looked at him in stunned surprise. She hadn't told him that she'd missed a period, hadn't wanted to get her hopes or his up about the possibility of a pregnancy.

"It's true," he said, his eyes shining with a brightness, a happiness that filled her up. "You're pregnant, Willa. We're going to have a little girl and she's already filled with a white spirit and a love that I can feel."

Tears filled Willa's eyes, happy tears and she laughed with joy as Jared stood and pulled her up to her feet and into his arms.

"It's all coming true for us, Willa. All the dreams I had when I was held captive, all the dreams you had for yourself. We have the fluffy loving dog and we're going to have a baby and we have each other."

"And love," she added. "We definitely have love."

He took her lips with his, the kiss speaking of the incredible love he had for her and stirring her own for him. The loneliness she'd once felt had been banished when he'd walked out of her dreams and into her life.

When the kiss ended he smiled down at her. "We need to plan a wedding," he said. "I'd like it to happen before our little one joins us."

Once again her heart trilled with joy. "You name the place and the time and I'll be there."

Once again his mouth took hers, this time with a simmering hunger. His hands pulled the tie from the nape of her neck to loosen her hair, then slid sensually down her back. *Do you know what I'm thinking?*

She broke the kiss and grinned at him. *I don't have to be a mind reader to know exactly what you're thinking.*

He grinned and scooped her up in his arms and carried her into the house and down the hallway toward the bedroom. It didn't matter that he had no past. She had his future and what a glorious future it was going to be.

* * * * *

*Harlequin Intrigue top author
Delores Fossen presents a brand-new series
of breathtaking romantic suspense!*
TEXAS MATERNITY: HOSTAGES
*The first installment available May 2010:
THE BABY'S GUARDIAN*

Shaw cursed and hooked his arm around Sabrina. Despite the urgency that the deadly gunfire created, he tried to be careful with her, and he took the brunt of the fall when he pulled her to the ground. His shoulder hit hard, but he held on tight to his gun so that it wouldn't be jarred from his hand.

Shaw didn't stop there. He crawled over Sabrina, sheltering her pregnant belly with his body, and he came up ready to return fire.

This was obviously a situation he'd wanted to avoid at all cost. He didn't want his baby in the middle of a fight with these armed fugitives, but when they fired that shot, they'd left him no choice. Now, the trick was to get Sabrina safely out of there.

"Get down," someone on the SWAT team yelled from the roof of the adjacent building.

Shaw did. He dropped lower, covering Sabrina as best he could.

There was another shot, but this one came from a rifleman on the SWAT team. Shaw didn't look up, but he heard the sound of glass being blown apart.

The shots continued, all coming from his men, which meant it might be time to try to get Sabrina to better cover. Shaw glanced at the front of the building.

So that Sabrina's pregnant belly wouldn't be smashed against the ground, Shaw eased off her and moved her to a sitting position so that her back was against the brick wall. They were close. Too close. And face-to-face.

He found himself staring right into those sea-green eyes.

How will Shaw get Sabrina out?
Follow the daring rescue and the heartbreaking
aftermath in THE BABY'S GUARDIAN
by Delores Fossen,
available May 2010
from Harlequin Intrigue.

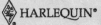

HARLEQUIN®

INTRIGUE

**BESTSELLING
HARLEQUIN INTRIGUE® AUTHOR**

DELORES FOSSEN

**PRESENTS AN ALL-NEW
THRILLING TRILOGY**

TEXAS MATERNITY:
HOSTAGES

When masked gunmen take over the maternity ward
at a San Antonio hospital, local cops, FBI and the scared
mothers can't figure out any possible motive. Before
long, secrets are revealed, and a city that has been on
edge since the siege began learns the truth behind the
negotiations and must deal with the fallout.

LOOK FOR

THE BABY'S GUARDIAN, *May*
DEVASTATING DADDY, *June*
THE MOMMY MYSTERY, *July*

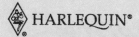
LAURA MARIE ALTOM

The Baby Twins

Stephanie Olmstead has her hands full raising
her twin baby girls on her own. When she runs
into old friend Brady Flynn, she's shocked to find
herself suddenly attracted to the handsome airline
pilot! Will this flyboy be the perfect daddy—
or will he crash and burn?

Love Inspired®

Former bad boy Sloan Hawkins is back in
Redemption, Oklahoma, to help keep his aunt's
cherished garden thriving and to reconnect with the
girl he left behind, Annie Markham. But when he
discovers his secret child—and that single mother
Annie never stopped loving him—he's determined
that a wedding will take place in the garden
nurtured by faith and love.

REDEMPTION
R I V E R

Where healing flows...

Look for

The Wedding Garden
by Linda Goodnight

*Available May 2010
wherever you buy books.*

Steeple
Hill®
LI87595

www.SteepleHill.com

LARGER-PRINT BOOKS!

GET 2 FREE LARGER-PRINT NOVELS

PLUS 2 FREE GIFTS!

HARLEQUIN®

INTRIGUE®

Breathtaking Romantic Suspense

HILP10R

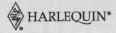

HARLEQUIN®

Showcase

On sale May 11, 2010

Reader favorites from the most talented voices in romance

Save $1.00 on the purchase of 1 or more Harlequin® Showcase books.

SAVE $1.00 on the purchase of 1 or more Harlequin® Showcase books.

Coupon expires Oct 31, 2010. Redeemable at participating retail outlets. Limit one coupon per purchase. Valid in the U.S.A. and Canada only.

52609015

Canadian Retailers: Harlequin Enterprises Limited will pay the face value of this coupon plus 10.25¢ if submitted by customer for this product only. Any other use constitutes fraud. Coupon is nonassignable. Void if taxed, prohibited or restricted by law. Consumer must pay any government taxes. Void if copied. Nielsen Clearing House ("NCH") customers submit coupons and proof of sales to Harlequin Enterprises Limited, P.O. Box 3000, Saint John, NB E2L 4L3, Canada. Non-NCH retailer—for reimbursement submit coupons and proof of sales directly to Harlequin Enterprises Limited, Retail Marketing Department, 225 Duncan Mill Rd., Don Mills, ON M3B 3K9, Canada.

U.S. Retailers: Harlequin Enterprises Limited will pay the face value of this coupon plus 8¢ if submitted by customer for this product only. Any other use constitutes fraud. Coupon is nonassignable. Void if taxed, prohibited or restricted by law. Consumer must pay any government taxes. Void if copied. For reimbursement submit coupons and proof of sales directly to Harlequin Enterprises Limited, P.O. Box 880478, El Paso, TX 88588-0478, U.S.A. Cash value 1/100 cents.

5 65373 00076 2 (8100)0 11651

® and TM are trademarks owned and used by the trademark owner and/or its licensee.
© 2009 Harlequin Enterprises Limited

HSCCOUP0410

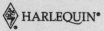 HARLEQUIN®

INTRIGUE

COMING NEXT MONTH

Available May 11, 2010

#1203 HER BODYGUARD
Bodyguard of the Month
Mallory Kane

#1204 HITCHED!
Whitehorse, Montana: Winchester Ranch
B.J. Daniels

#1205 THE BABY'S GUARDIAN
Texas Maternity: Hostages
Delores Fossen

#1206 STRANDED WITH THE PRINCE
Defending the Crown
Dana Marton

#1207 STRANGER IN A SMALL TOWN
Shivers
Kerry Connor

#1208 MAN UNDERCOVER
Thriller
Alana Matthews